UNI
MOUN'
(And the F

Written by Larry and Michelle Portch

Illustrations by Stilson Greene

Photos by Larry Portch and Cody Shreiner

Edited by Janet Witkowski and Heidi Todd

–

2

Acknowledgements

I would like to thank my friends and family for their support and help in making this book possible. In particular, I am thankful for the permission given to use many of the family and friends' names that were used for characters within the book.

The characters in this book are fictitious and in no way reflect their real life counterparts. The use of these names is in no way intended to degrade or diminish individuals, personally. Although their names, due to historical ancestral references of long ago were used, this story and particular details and characters are completely fictionalized.

PROLOGUE

It could be said that sometimes when our country has had a very cold fall that the destiny of our country can be very much in question, or is it just my destiny. Oh, well, as to whether it is actually the weather, the season or the place, I cannot say. I do know that whether it is 1862 or 1982, fall has always had a strange way of leaving me quite unsettled. Oh, I know you might question my reasoning, but just listen to my story and you may begin to understand why the cold fall of the year 1862 has effected every cold fall I will ever have. You see, it all started with my hobby. Well, my hobby, my friends, my kids, and oh yes, my wife. Maybe my hobby became just a little excessive—just a little—but everyone needs a good hobby. I just didn't need my friends, ghosts or superstitions to work on my already 'over the top' imagination. My hobby, to my wife's chagrin, took a lot of research, which I will admit can become totally self-absorbing. This causes one to lose some sense of reality. Well, maybe reality is what is to be questioned, maybe. Or maybe, after reading this, you'll question your own reality.

You see, my hobby is metal detecting. Specifically, I do metal detecting for Civil War artifacts. Where I live and the places I go have set still in time for over 100 years with stone-wall lined roads, very old plantations, old mills and places way back in the

—

woods where people have not stepped for a century and a half. Yes, the last people to have touched these hallow grounds were Civil War soldiers. The only thing left is their artifacts, bullets, unexploded shells and their spirits. Yeah, that's one of my problems; having their personal belongings in my hand, the feel, the smell, and the sounds of those doggone spirits.

Oh yes, did I mention the danger from unexploded artillery shells, cased bullets and ghosts that scream at you to put it back? Ugh! Oh yeah, ghosts.

I know that some of your fathers have hobbies, and you can see how they can become totally self-absorbed. Perhaps they have not ever included you in their exploits, and you have felt left out. If not, possibly your moms have felt left out.

I suppose I knew I might have a problem when people would ask for directions to some place or another, and I would give them names of places that have not existed for over one hundred years. Actually, now that I think of it, it did not start with my hobby. It started with one of my best friend's great grandfathers. That's where the year 1862 comes in. It was a very cold fall. A very cold fall and Jay Seaton was privileged to be there. Right there, while my most favorite thing in the whole world was happening—history, oh yes, history.

I know you're not interested in history, but maybe, just maybe, you will be now. I am sure that if you listen, listen real hard, you can hear them. Just listen. Take a whiff of the crisp air. Can't you smell the smoke of the campfires? Can't you see them? Can't you feel them? Just listen, listen real hard. If you live where I do, you surely could.

"Good morning, General Stuart, good morning, sir."

"Have a good night's sleep last night, Jeb?"

"Yes sir. Seen General Jackson anywhere?"

Oh. Maybe I'm getting a little ahead of myself, or maybe I went too far back in history too fast. Let's fast-forward to 1982 where my story begins. Grab onto your seats, hold onto your hats, and let's just take a little more modern ride back into history...

UNISON DAY IS A COMIN

(Chapter 1)

Grandma Craun is baking pies in the kitchen at the Craun Family Farmhouse. It is early morning, and four kids come charging into the kitchen all excited for the day's festivities. Cody Craun, a handsome thirteen-year-old boy, leads the procession. Cody has dark wavy hair, is tall and thin and seems to be the leader of the crew. Heather Stuart enters next cutting in front of Cody. She has long red hair and dark green eyes. She is a very pretty young girl, but a tomboy through and through. Cubby Seaton comes bolting through the door into the kitchen and slides into the counter, knocking the flour jar into the freshly baked cookies.

"Cubby!" Grandma Craun exclaims. "What are you doing?" Cubby is ten years old, and rather clumsy. He's a little on the pudgy side too, but very athletic.

"Grandma, can I have a cookie?" asks Cubby enthusiastically. All the neighborhood children call her Grandma.

"No, honey, they're for the bazaar. You'll have to wait till tomorrow."

Heather stares at the pumpkin pie, longingly, rocking back and forth on her heels. Sean, Heather's younger brother, who has been watching this spectacle shyly says, "Just a couple?"

"Cody, you take this crew of confederate banshees," says Grandma, "and get them out of my kitchen."

Heather asks Grandma, "Can I help?"

"Why thank you, Heather," says Grandma as she turns her back looking for something Heather can do. "Let me see..."

While Grandma is contemplating her dilemma, Cody picks up the pumpkin pie and moves briskly towards the kitchen door.

"Heather – why don't you go to the pantry and get me a jar of canned cherries," Grandma finally decides.

Cody turns and signals the crew of confederate banshees to follow him. Cubby quickly turns to follow Cody, and knocks the cookies on the kitchen floor. All of the kids freeze.

Grandma Craun hollers, "That's it, get out! Get out of my kitchen!"

All four confederate banshees speed across the pasture to enjoy their ill-gotten gain– the pumpkin pie. The kids scramble into the Craun's old red barn where all the children keep their horses to escape from being caught. They jump into the hay, while Cody holds the pie high above his head to protect it. But Cubby trips over his two feet, knocking Cody over, and landing face first into the pie.

"Cubby!" Cody yelps.

"I'm sorry," exclaims Cubby.

"Oh, well. At least we'll have part of the pie," says Cody.

—
8

Sean tries to lighten the mood, "Let's go to the clubhouse and we can share what's left of the pie."

Heather gets up and walks over to her horse, Shadow, and stroking her mane says, "Shadow, how are you doing today?" Shadow is a silver-gray mare with a long silver mane and tail. She means the world to Heather who got Shadow for her birthday three years ago.

Sean barks at Heather, "Why don't you leave that doggone horse alone?" Sean likes to taunt her. He's smart, quick witted, and sharp tongued, much to Heather's chagrin.

Cody stands up for Heather, "Sean, you like Tramp as much as she likes Shadow – Leave her alone."

Sean says, "Yeah, yeah, yeah, you're always sticking up for her. Why do we have a girl in our group anyway? Let's go to the clubhouse." The clubhouse is located on the top floor of the Unison Store where Cubby's father Doug is the proprietor. Sean picks up the pie and starts to run across the fields toward town, followed closely behind by Cubby.

Heather says, "Oh no, you're not going to try and leave me behind. I can do anything you can do."

"Oh come on, Heather," replies Cody, "I want some pie."

As the four children get closer to the Unison Store, Cubby hollers out, "We need forks, we need forks!"

The four kids stumble into the front door of Unison Country Store. Cubby's dad's love for the Civil War spilled over into the store's flavor. There were old-fashioned candy counters, a potbelly stove, 19th century shelving, and Civil War artifacts, maps and décor that gave the visitors to his store the sensation that they had just stepped back into time.

Doug says, "Whoa, not in the store. Out – out – you kid's get out!"

"Dad, we need a drink," says Cubby.

Cubby grabbing sodas off the shelf, Mr. Seaton bellows, "You're not eating up my store profits. Get out of here!"

The four kids slam out the door and head to the rear stairs of the store to the second floor where their clubhouse is located. In their hand are their ill-gotten gains. The kids quietly and sneakily work their way up the stairs to their clubhouse, being careful not to let the door squeak too much so Cubby's dad doesn't know they have entered their secret hideaway. There the four confederate banshees share and devour their pumpkin pie and sodas that they obtained on their morning escapades. Sean looks through the cracks in the floor to observe what is going on that day in the store. While the kid's secret clubhouse was upstairs, the father's headquarters was downstairs.

There, around the potbelly stove, everyone's favorite place to hang out, playing checkers was Old Man Carter, George Delaney, and Josh Willis. These three men were regulars at the country store and are generally

---

considered to be the authority on the history of the area. George Delaney is an ancestor of the Old Welbourne estate. Old Man Carter is the resident historian of the local hearsay about the Civil War, and Josh is an old retired preacher who used to head the congregation of Delaney's Chapel. Josh was a son of a first generation of Civil War slaves from the plantations in and around Unison, VA during the Civil War. Doug Seaton was the great grandson of Jay Seaton, who was one of Colonial John Singleton Moby's Confederate Rangers during the Civil War. Mr. Seaton, because of family stories and diaries had good access to information about the Civil War and was a devout metal detector enthusiast that had a passion for locating, searching and finding Civil Wars artifacts. In his pursuit of his hobby, he had two cohorts: Cody's dad, Ronnie Craun, and Heather and Sean's dad, John Stuart. The kids loved to listen to the old men's stories as they fought and argued all day over what happened over a hundred years ago. It should be noted that their recollections of what happened during the Civil War bared little resemblance to what actually happened during the Civil War. However, it kept up a lively debate between them and the fathers of the four confederate banshees.

The kids have become fascinated with Old Man Carter's story about the Battle of Unison. All four of them have their own secret spying location in the cracks of the old store's planks in the floor. Suddenly, the kids hear the Dixie song being whistled and see that Cody's

Cody's dad is standing outside the front door with a smirk on his face, proudly holding a Union belt buckle.

Doug suspiciously asks, "Where have you been without me?"

"You know where I've been."

"You're not supposed to go there without me," retorts Doug.

"Well then," Mr. Craun starts to reply.

But just then Mr. Stuart enters behind Ronnie asking, "Go where without who? What are you two up to?" Mr. Stuart, much to his regret, works in the city, and is consistently missing out on metal detecting opportunities.

Doug sharply replies, "Nowhere."

Mr. Stuart says, "What's going on?"

Mrs. Betty Beavers, one of the ladies working on the Unison festivities, breaks into the conversation as she swishes her way into the store, "We need help at the church. You three need to help us set up tables for the bazaar for Unison Day. Furthermore, there are three people looking for you claiming that they are historians."

Mr. Craun quickly puts the belt buckle in his pocket and says to John, "Not now. We'll tell you later."

"I can't leave the store until Mrs. Connors shows up to take my place." Mr. Seaton says.

Mrs. Beavers answers, "Don't worry. She's right behind me. You need to get going."

The four kids, realizing that the excitement was now moving to the church decided to head down there as well.

———

UNISON'S BIG DAY

(Chapter 2)

In 1862 and 1863, Unison Church and the home of Five Oaks had been used as a hospital during the Civil War. Unison Day was a fall festival held to make money to support the village of Unison and its church. This year the church elders decided to incorporate some Civil War history at the festival to try to bring in larger crowds for the festival. The church asked the fathers of those confederate banshees to set up an archeological display and bring in a re-enactment group for Unison Day, playing off of the old hospital story.

The fathers had contacted the 8th Virginia Artillery Group to set up a pretend camp and cannons to entertain the festival participants. As the kids exited the store towards the church, they saw a truck full of men dressed in Confederate uniforms pull up in the store parking lot. Sean says, "There are the Confederate soldiers."

One of the men hollers out the window to the kids, "Hey kids, you wouldn't happen to know where we're to set up camp at, would you?"

Cody immediately answers, "Yeah, I'll get you there." Cody and the kids jump into the back of their pickup truck, and Cody shows them to the field across the street from Unison Church.

Cubby is fascinated by the buttons on their uniforms. "Wow. My dad has buttons just like that."

One of the re-enactors asks, "Where did your dad get the buttons from?"

Cubby retorts, "Out of the ground."

Another of the re-enactors says, "Oh, your dad metal detects?"

Cody chimes in, "Yeah, all of our dads' metal detect, but would I ever like to wear a confederate uniform like you have."

"Well, if you help us set up the camp, we'll see what we can do about getting you uniforms," said the man. Cody and Sean shared their dad's passion for the Civil War, and thought it would be cool to be dressed in Confederate uniforms for Unison Day.

Sean enthusiastically says, "Oh, yeah, thank you. We have to ask our dads."

Cody says, "We'll be right back."

As the kids scamper off to the church to ask permission, the kids run into the church, skip up the stairs and into the balcony where they could hear their fathers talking to the historians from the Smithsonian Institute. "Dad, dad!" hollers Sean.

"Quiet Sean, wait a minute."

Cubby says, "But dad."

"You kids be quiet a minute," growls Mr. Seaton, "We're almost done here."

The engrossed conversation between the kid's fathers and the preservationist was on how to save Civil War graffiti that had been placed on the walls of the church by wounded Union soldiers during the Civil War. Fortunately, the graffiti had been written in lead pencil and the preservationists told them that they could just strip the paint and put a glass cover over the graffiti to save it. But the kids were in no mood and had no patience to hear the preservationist's instructions to the parents on how this was to be done. And out of Cody's mouth comes, "Dad – they want us to help set up their camp. Can we?"

Mr. Craun says, "Go ask your mother."

The kids scamper down the steps and out onto the church lawn where their mothers were setting up the tables and getting ready for the church bazaar. "Mom, mom, the soldiers want us to help them set up their camp. Can we?" asks Heather.

Mrs. Stuart, who is a pretty lady with brownish, red hair and dark green eyes, is anxious to finally see the kids, "I thought you kids were supposed to be here setting up the tables and helping with the bazaar."

"But mom," says Sean, "They're going to let us wear uniforms."

"You want to wear what?" asks Mrs. Stuart.

"Uniforms, mom," hollers Sean, "Uniforms."

Mrs. Stuart, who is a little tired from all of the preparations retorts, "Civil War, Civil War. All I hear is Civil War. Go ask your father."

The kid's let out a collective sigh and then turn around scrambling back into the church and hollering up to the balcony from the floor of the church, "Dad, dad!"

The kids try to get more out, but Mr. Craun bellows, "You kids need to go find something to do!"

With that the four banshees run out of the church, cross the street passing by their mothers and off to the field. Cody says, "Ok – they said we could do it, right?"

Heather says, "That's what I heard." The kids spend the rest of the afternoon setting up the Confederate Camp. As the day wore on, more and more re-enactors showed up and the camp grew and grew with more and more re-enactors dressed in period clothing. There were horses and wagons, men dressed as sutlers selling old fashioned hair brushes and mirrors, men dressed as blacksmiths, women dressed in fancy antebellum dresses, and children dressed in the play clothes of the time. By mid-afternoon, what had started out as an empty field in itself became a small town. Buddy, who had promised the uniforms to the kids earlier that morning, managed to find pants, hats, and shirts for all three of the boys. But Buddy, could not seem to find a fourth uniform for Heather. Heather was beside herself with disappointment. The boys looked like quite a sight, as the clothes are not exactly a perfect fit; being a tad on the large size. The kids sprint over to the concessions area at the church to show off their new found digs to their moms who are setting up the tables. They had been working all day in the hot sun, so they were anxious to get something to drink and maybe some ice cream.

—

Sean struts up to his mom and announces, "Hey mom. Can we have something to drink?"

Mrs. Stuart looks up abashed to find her son and his friends in their confederate attire, "Oh, my goodness. Look at you. Where did you ever get those uniforms?"

Heather huffs in, "They got them from some of the Civil War re-enactors." Mrs. Stuart starts handing the kids sodas, while Heather pouts in the chair at the end of the table. "He ran out of uniforms, when it came to me," sighs Heather.

"You're a girl, anyway," retorts Cubby.

"So?" snips Heather.

Mrs. Craun has been listening to this banter and added, "You know, I have one of Cody's Great Grandmother's dresses in a trunk in the attic. I have a funny feeling that it might fit you perfectly."

"Really?" asks Heather.

All of a sudden, Buddy, comes up to the concessions table and introduces himself to Mrs. Stuart and Mrs. Craun saying, "Sorry I couldn't find a uniform for Heather."

Mrs. Craun answers, "That's all right. I think we found a solution."

Buddy says, "Oh good, because I thought maybe the kids, if you'd let them and maybe yourselves would like to attend our party tonight. Everyone is going to dress up in period clothes; there will be plenty of music, campfires, songs and dancing. Would you be interested?"

The kids all let out an emphatic, "Yes!"

17

Mrs. Stuart replies, "Well, we have a lot to do tonight for the bazaar, but I'm sure that the kids and their fathers would love to come."

Mrs. Craun agrees, "Sounds like fun."

"But mom," says Heather, "What about my dress?"

Mrs. Craun explains, "We've got a little time. Why don't you come with me?" Mrs. Craun and Heather leave with excitement to go work on finding the period dress.

Buddy says, "I need to get with Mr. Seaton, because we don't have room for the medical group re-enactors to set up. There's no more space."

Mrs. Stuart says, "Well, I believe they're up in the balcony of the church."

"Come on," says Cody, We'll take you." With sodas in hand, the kids scamper up the church steps to the balcony where the fathers have been setting up their Civil War displays.

"Dad, dad," says Sean.

Mr. Stuart jokes, "Whoa, three confederate soldiers." Buddy explains to Mr. Seaton that there is a lack of space in the field, and finds that they need a place for the medical re-enactors to set up.

Mr. Craun says, "Well, what about Five Oaks? That's where the medical camp was anyway."

Buddy asks, "You know about what happened here?"

Mr. Seaton sarcastically announces, "Just a little."

Buddy asks, "What are you doing, here?"

—

18

Mr. Stuart replies, "Helping the church preserve the graffiti left on the walls by the Union soldiers."

Buddy looks at the writing on the walls and then turns and looks at the artifacts on the table. He asks, "Are these artifacts, yours?"

Mr. Craun replies, "Yep."

Buddy asks, "You don't happen to have some original 8th Virginia Artillery Buttons, do you?"

Mr. Stuart says, "Uh, probably."

"Well, I'd trade a handful of buttons for three uniforms."

Mr. Stuart retorts, "Well, I don't know..."

"Dad!" Sean exclaims.

"Oh, we'll see what we can do," Mr. Stuart looks at the other fathers finding Mr. Seaton shaking his head emphatically no.

Mr. Craun says to Buddy, "Come on, I'll take you over to Five Oaks to see if Mrs. Edwards will let you set up a camp in her yard."

Eileen Edwards is a tall, lanky, slender woman who moved to the country because of her interest in the antebellum period. She loves the pomp and splendor of what she believes is plantation life, and chose to leave the boring city life to relive her fantasies of her views of a better life. The men find her downstairs dressed in a beautiful pink antebellum dress. She has appointed herself as the Unison Day storyteller, and has a group of young children gathered around her as she is telling a plantation story about life in the old days. She is in her element, and the kids are excited to listen as she uses her exaggerated southern accent.

Mr. Craun interrupts, "Mrs. Edwards, this is Buddy. We have another re-enactment group coming in. Would you mind if they camped in amongst the oaks at Five Oaks? It's where the original medical camp was, anyway. It would work out real well."

Mrs. Edwards, who is extremely enthusiastic about Unison Day and the Civil War replies, "Really, ah, there was a medical camp on my property? No wonder I've been seeing ghosts."

Buddy asks, "It really was a medical camp?"

Mr. Craun replies, "Oh! Yeah! Why don't you go read some of those poems on the wall of the church?"

Mrs. Edwards says, "There are poems on the walls of the church about my Five Oaks?"

Mr. Craun regretting his leak of information replies, "Well, not about Five Oaks, and I don't think you should go read those poems."

Mrs. Edwards asks, "Why ever not?"

"How do I say this – The stuff written on the walls is not – exactly appropriate."

Mrs. Edwards gives a shocked but understanding look as she changes the subject back to the re-enactors, "Now, you're not going to mess up my property, are you?"

Mr. Craun eases her mind, "Oh no, everything will be fine. It's just tents."

Mr. Craun eases her mind, "Oh no, everything will be fine. It's just tents." Mrs. Edwards agrees to let the re-enactors set up tent on her property and goes back to her story telling.

As Mr. Craun and Buddy start to walk away, Buddy says, "You know they're going to want to build a fire, right? That's ok –isn't it?"

"Oh yeah, make it a big one," says Mr. Craun sarcastically.

During this interaction between Mrs. Edwards, Mr. Craun, and Buddy the three remaining banshees have been running in and amongst the tables creating a fuss and causing pandemonium. Poor Cubby trips over his pants as he's grabbing for a cupcake and hits the end of the table causing the two end legs to buckle which makes the pies and cakes start to slide down the table. Cody quickly grabs the end of the table before all is lost, saving the day. Mrs. Stuart and Mrs. Seaton fly over to those banshees. Mrs. Stuart exclaims, "Look at you. You come with me back to the house so we can pin those clothes up. You are a sight."

Buddy, who was walking by, over hears the conversation, and responds to Mrs. Stuart, "You can go ahead and sew them to fit – I have my 8th Virginia original buttons."

Grandma Craun, who has been watching this spectacle says, "Why don't you let them come with me, we can ride over to the farm, get them something decent to eat and make them a little more presentable."

CAMP LIFE

(Chapter 3)

The farmhouse had been in the Craun family for generations. It was an old 1830's – 1850's style two-story white farmhouse that had been renovated and brought up to modern standards. The barns, carriage house, stables and smoke house still gave the feel of stepping back into history. The boys and Grandma Craun enter into the kitchen ready to devour whatever they can put together for food. Cody is starving and hollers out through the house to his mom, "Mom, mom, I'm hungry." Up in the attic Mrs. Craun who is just putting the finishing touches on Heather's ensemble spins her around to take a good look at her. Heather was in a beautiful emerald green antebellum dress that uncannily brought out the green sparkle in her eyes. The dress was trimmed with lace and red bows that lined the base of the bottom of the hoop. The dress was short sleeved with a low neckline. Mrs. Craun had carefully placed her hair up, as was the style of the time, Heather's naturally curly hair laid in wisps around her face making her stunning to behold. For finishing touches Mrs. Craun had placed a green choker of ribbon around her neck, and given her a small purse that matched the green in the dress.

Mrs. Craun admired her creation, taking Heather to a full-length mirror and saying, "Look Heather, you're beautiful."

Heather steps back and gasps, amazed at her own beauty. Then she thinks for a second and responds, "Yeah, but I wanted to wear a uniform."

Cody comes to the bottom of the attic steps, irate that he has not gotten a response, "Mom, you up there?"

Mrs. Craun replies, "We'll be right down. I don't see how you could possibly still be hungry." Cody starts up the stairs, but pauses as he sees Heather gliding down the steps. Cody is momentarily awestricken and shocked by Heather. Cody freezes in his steps creating a long moment of silence. Mrs. Craun says, breaking the moment of silence, "Ok, Heather. Let's go show Grandma." Cody is still frozen in his steps as Mrs. Craun says, "Cody, I thought you were hungry. You need to turn around and go down the steps so we can get to the kitchen." Cody turns and heads down the steps to the kitchen. Mrs. Craun softly takes Heather by the shoulders and guides her to Grandma.

"Grandma," says Mrs. Craun, "Who does this look like?"

"Oh my goodness, Heather, you are beautiful," exclaims Grandma, "You're the spitting image of my mother. You will be the belle of the ball."

Cubby annoyed by this whole spectacle hollers, "Heather is a girly girl. Heather is a girly girl."

Mrs. Craun asks, "Sean, do you want to stay here or do you and Heather want to go home to eat?"

23

Heather pipes in, "Can we eat here?"

"I would like to stay, too," replies Sean. Mrs. Craun hands the phone from the counter to Heather who calls her mom for permission.

Cubby looks like he is about to ask to stay, when Mrs. Craun interrupts him and says, "I know you're staying Cubby."

While Mrs. Craun fixes dinner, Grandma Craun goes to the corner to get her sewing basket and needle telling, "Cubby, you need to come over here and get those pants sewn up. You can't stand up on your own two feet when you're pants are the right length let alone dragging under the bottom of your shoes."

"Ha! Ha! Now who's the girly girl," retorts Sean.

Grandma replies, "Don't worry Sean, you're next." Grandma commences to fix the uniforms so that all three confederate banshees are totally presentable, looking as if they had just stepped back into time.

After dinner, Mrs. Stuart pulls up to the Craun house and Heather bolts out the door to show off her new dress to her mother. Mrs. Stuart gets her first good look at Heather and says, "Heather, you look stunning. Wait till your father sees you."

"Mom, can I ride Shadow over to the church?" asks Heather.

"Oh, Heather," replies Mrs. Stuart, "Why don't you get in the car, and I'll drive you all over."

"But mom," begs Heather.

—

Mrs. Craun breaks in, "Heather, the horses have to be groomed, saddled and wiped down. It's too much for tonight, and I still have things to do if your mom might help me out we can be done in an hour and head over to the camp. Why don't you kids walk across the pasture to the church and bother your fathers for a while."

Sean says, "Ok. Come on – it's getting dark, and I want to go by that graveyard before the sun goes down."

The kids head across the pasture towards the church, and past the pond towards the old graveyard. The graveyard stood by the first Friend's Meeting Church in the middle of the pasture beyond the pond behind Five Oaks. All four of the kids were positive it was haunted, because of listening to their father's tales. The kids, having a deep respect for their dads, and not believing their fathers to lie, did not want to be caught in that graveyard after dark. So with swift feet, they quickly passed the graveyard and darted for the church.

When the kids arrived at the camp, they found the campfires burning high and the smell of hot dogs and hamburgers filling the air. Buddy is sitting around one of the campfires telling stories to some of the guests. Cody sees his dad in the center of the camp talking to some of the re-enactors.

Cody and the kids run up to them and say, "Hey dad."

Mr. Stuart, noticing Heather, says, "Oh, my gosh, Heather."

Then Buddy comes up behind the kids saying, "Oh my, what a difference. You look like you belong here. Want to join a re-enactment group?" The four kids sit down and grab some of the marshmallows sitting on the bench and commence to start roasting marshmallows and settle down to their favorite past time of listening to old Civil War stories. Sitting around the campfire could also be found George Delaney, Old Man Carter and Josh Willis. The old men were loudly debating what they commonly knew as the Battle of Union and Bloomfield.

Buddy pipes in asking, "Where's Union?"

Mr. Seaton replies, "Here – it was called Union during the Civil War. Sometime after the war, there were too many Union, Virginias, so the post office made them change their name. The town decided to change it to Unison."

"Did what these old men say, actually happen here?" asks Buddy.

"Somewhat," says Mr. Stuart.

"Well, where's Bloomfield?" asks Buddy.

"About two miles west of here," says Mr. Craun.

Mr. Seaton chimes in, "You mean to say that you don't know the history of your own unit?"

"Well, yes and no. We were given directions here, but we never heard of Union, so what did happen here?" asks Buddy.

Mr. Seaton, who loves to tell this story, starts the tale, "According to the Official Records, and not those three old codgers over there, General Stuart was camped between here

—

26

and Bloomfield. We believe they stayed at a place called Old Welbourne – halfway between here and Bloomfield. Alfred Pleasonton, a Union Calvary Commander, was at Philomont."

"Where's Philomont?" asks Buddy.

"Well, it's up the road in front of the church, about 3 miles from here – northeast of town," said Mr. Seaton. "Anyway, to make things simple. The Union Army was advancing up this road towards this town, and parts of General Stuart's troops were in the woods a mile and a half on this road between Union and Philomont. There, the first clash of the two cavalries hit, and they gradually fought a series of skirmishes up this road to about a mile to a mile and a half from where we're standing to a place called Seaton's Hill."

"Well, that's your last name, isn't it?" asks Buddy.

"Yeah, it was part of my great grandfather's farm," replies Mr. Seaton.

"So, your families have been here a long time?"

"Yes, for generations."

"So was your grandfather in the Civil War?" asks Buddy.

"Yeah, he was one of John Mosby's men."

"Well, was he in this battle?" asks Buddy.

"Well, it really wasn't a battle it was just skirmish lines and Mosby's Rangers hadn't been formed yet."

"Do you have a picture of your great grandfather?" asks Buddy.

Mr. Craun jokes, "You're looking at him."

—

27

"What do you mean?" inquires Buddy.

"Well, we have a book on John Mosby's Rangers, and in the book is a picture of Jay Seaton, who's Doug's Great Grandfather," replies Mr. Craun, "And Doug Seaton is the spitting image of his Great Grandfather." Doug looks rather sheepish about the comment. Buddy starts to laugh. "Oh, you think that's something," says Mr. Craun, "John, is the spitting image of John Mosby. So it looks like they are both in the picture."

"Well where were you?" asks Buddy.

"I wasn't there," said Mr. Craun.

"Well, did you have relatives in the war?"

"Not that I know of," says Ronnie.

Doug says, "Yeah right. Anyway – You want to know about your unit, or not."

"Well, yeah," replies Buddy.

"Well, your Battery was attached to General Stuart and under Major Pelham," says Doug.

"Well, where were they?" asks Buddy.

"On this road heading northeast on a hill over Beaver Dam Creek," says Mr. Seaton.

"And you know where this hill's at?" asks Buddy.

"Oh, yes. There's an artillery redoubt there."

"Well, were there a lot of losses here?" asks Buddy.

"No, not really, and the Official Records don't give too accurate an account of the missing, wounded and killed in action."

"Well, that's cool," says Buddy, "Who won?"

"Well it depends," replies Mr. Seaton, "It depends! There were three or four separate actions and it depends on which one you want to talk about – but in general, General Stuart's orders were just to stop the Union Army from getting through the mountain passes, of which he did." And he was facing the whole Union Army with less than 1200 men. So he eventually pulled on out and moved south."

Buddy asks, "So – did my buttons come from here?"

"No," says Mr. Stuart, "Most of them came from Aldie."

"But these are real buttons?"

"Oh, yeah," says Mr. Stuart, "All 36 of them."

Buddy asks, "Well, what about the church – was it used as a hospital?"

"No, not for this battle," says Mr. Craun, "That was another year, another movement."

"So, they were here more than once?" asks Buddy.

"Yeah," Mr. Seaton replies. "Well, I'd like to thank you for the buttons. We try real hard to have the actual artifacts on our uniform, and they're very hard to find."

All three of the fathers reply, "We know."

Mrs. Stuart and Mrs. Craun come up to the men, "Civil War, Civil War, and Civil War! Why don't you take me to look around? Have you seen your daughter?"

"Yeah. Well, they were here just a second ago. Where did she get the dress from?" asks Mr. Stuart.

Mrs. Craun says, "It was my great grandmothers. Come on Ronnie, we need to go look at some stuff, too."

Off in the backside of the camp the battalion band was playing old historic ballads of the period. Over the band could be heard the swing of the blacksmith's anvil and large bellow of air purging into his forge. Far off in a quiet corner could be found storytellers giving explanations of how things were done in that period of time – but none of the kids could be found. After taking in most of the sights, the Crauns and Stuarts bump into each other, and Mrs. Craun asks the Stuarts if they had seen the kids. "No," says Mrs. Stuart, "And we've been just about everywhere."

"Did you check the stables?" asks Mr. Craun. "You know how they are with horses."

Mr. Stuart replies, "Yes, we passed through there. They're not there."

"What about the medical camp at Five Oaks?" asks Mr. Craun.

Both mothers exclaim, "Eileen Edwards!"

"She was here just a bit ago – all dressed up," says Mrs. Stuart.

Meanwhile, over at Five Oaks, Mrs. Edwards has all the children gathered around a campfire as she tells her tales of the haunting of Five Oaks. She is dressed in another bright red antebellum dress with long white gloves. As usual, she is completely involved and excited

—

with the attention. Mr. Seaton is sitting on a log just as engrossed with the stories as the kids. Mrs. Edwards is thoroughly convinced that Five Oaks is haunted. The woman is beside herself with fear with every swish of a tree limb, screeching of a door, or bang in the night. She believes with all her heart in ghosts. The kids are encouraging Mr. Seaton to tell his story of the ghost of the graveyard behind Five Oaks. Mr. Seaton, giving his sheepish grin, begins to spill a wild yarn of an early eighteenth century tale from his vivid imagination when out of Mrs. Edwards mouth comes, "Oh my gosh, I told you this place was haunted."

In the meantime, the Stuarts and the Crauns had quietly appeared, standing in the back listening to the conversation. Mrs. Stuart finally says, "Quit telling those kids ghost stories. There's no such thing as a ghost."

"Not according to Doug," says Mr. Craun, "He's got his own ghost that follows him around in his car."

Mrs. Seaton who has been sitting at the campfire with Cubby on her lap says, "Oh, that's right." Mrs. Seaton has bright red hair, and is from a rather well to do family. She loves to mock her husband's superstitious beliefs in the afterworld.

Mr. Stuart asks, "What are you talking about?"

"Oh, that's right," says Mr. Craun, "We haven't told you yet."

"Told me what?" asks Mr. Stuart.

31

"Well, we believe we've specifically located the second to the last line of battle on Seaton's Hill," said Mr. Craun.

"Without me?" asks Mr. Stuart.

Mr. Craun replies, "Well, we were going to take you. You weren't around."

Mrs. Edwards asks, "What ghost?"

"Oh, you aren't going to believe this one," says Mrs. Seaton.

"Ok, Doug," asks Mr. Stuart. "What's going on?"

"Yeah, Doug," says Mr. Craun, "What's going on?"

"You got the big mouth," says Doug. "You tell it."

"Come on Mr. Craun," encourages Mrs. Edwards, "What happened. I told you there were ghosts."

"Well, I don't know about there being ghosts," replies Mr. Craun, "But good old Doug not only believes there's ghosts, but believes he can communicate with them and tell them what to do."

"Go ahead;" says Doug, "I'll get you back."

"Ok, ok, you two," says Mr. Stuart, "What's going on?"

"Well, it appears Doug went sneaking out metal detecting at night," replies Mr. Craun, "He wasn't going to tell you, and he wasn't going to tell me. But in payment he lost his favorite digging tool and the spirit world wasn't going to let him have it back."

"What are you talking about?" asks Mr. Stuart.

"Go ahead, Doug," says Mr. Craun, "Tell him."

Mrs. Craun, laughing says, "Go ahead, and tell him."

Cody now is really interested in the story, as are the other kids, and says, "Yeah, come on Mr. Seaton, what happened?" Mr. Seaton bawks, "You got the big mouth, Ronnie, you tell them."

"Well, I tried to get you to tell it your way," replies Mr. Craun. "If you aren't going to tell them, I will." So with that, Mr. Seaton briskly gets up and walks away from the fire.

"Well, for goodness sake," says Mrs. Edwards, "Somebody tell us what happened?"

"Ok," Mr. Craun says, "Like I said, Doug went metal detecting without us at night. There's a big tree up on Seaton's Hill that Doug had a good signal with his metal detector, but it was too dark for him to dig it. He thought he'd come back in the morning and get it, but when he got back in the car he realized his shovel was gone. So – he goes to get out of the car and he swears up and down somebody was holding the car door closed on him. He sat in the car for a few minutes and determined it was his imagination, so he tries again to get out of the car. He then forces his way out of the car having a battle with his imaginary friend with the door. He finally gives up and starts to drive back to the house. On the way home, he swears up and down that his imaginary friend is riding in the back seat of

———

33

the car with his knees pushing into the driver's seat. By the time he gets home, he has his car seat pulled all the way up to the steering wheel and swears up and down there are two knees being pushed through the seat into his back as hard as they could be pushed. He forces his way out of the car, looks into the back seat to see who's there, and with a loud voice tells his ghost, "I don't care who you are, I don't care what you want, and I am going back anyway." He slams the door shut and runs into the house."

Mrs. Seaton exclaims, "That's right. He was as white as a sheet. He had the shakes for hours."

"Doug told you this?" asks Mr. Stuart.

"Oh, yeah," says Mr. Craun, "He shows up at 2:00 AM in the morning and demands that I go with him. I insist he's drunk – he insists that I get in the car. He takes me to his camp, tells me to get out, and asks me, "Now what do you feel?" I told him I don't feel a doggone thing. He insists that I ought to be seeing his ghost. Finally, I asked where he was when he thought he came in contact with his ghost. He indicated that it was by a big tree at the top of the hill."

Mr. Craun looks toward Mr. Stuart, "So – you wanted to know what we were talking about this morning." Mr. Craun reached in his pocket and holds up the belt buckle that he showed Mr. Seaton this morning. This is what came from that big tree.

"Well, may I have a ghost follow me around for the rest of my life," says Mr. Stuart.

—

"I told you there are ghosts," says Mrs. Edwards, "I told you there's ghosts."

"Eileen," said Mrs. Stuart, "You and Doug have got to get over your crazy superstitions. Now kids, there are no such things as ghosts."

"Not according to Doug," says Mr. Craun.

"Ronnie you stop it," says Mrs. Craun, "You're going to have these kids up all night. We've got a big day tomorrow. It's time to take these kids home." With that, not one confederate banshee got any sleep that night from the bumps in the night and the spirits in their dreams.

THE NEXT DAY

(Chapter 4)

Unison Day comes and goes with little mention of ghosts and goblins. The four confederate banshees, while gorging themselves with food and blending in with the camp characters, ran around all day till they had totally worn themselves out. They decided to retire to their clubhouse. Their mothers had their hands full working the bazaar, and their fathers told stories of Unison Church and its involvement in the war till late afternoon when they packaged up their artifacts and returned them to the store. As all good fortune of little spies would have it, three figures appeared in the bottom of the store having the appearance of three army officers reviewing their maps and strategy. To the children's amazement, in full detail, with full illustrations, came their father's new excursion into the metal detecting world. Clearly heard was, "Mountsville."

"Mountsville?" says Sean, "We know where Mountsville's at. Why don't we go metal detecting at Mountsville?"

"One, they're never going to let us near those metal detectors," replies Cody, "And two, what Unfrequented Road? We'd have to get those maps."

Heather shushes Cody, "Be quiet, they'll hear us. Listen to what they're saying."

The three fathers are heavy into their debate over where the battle of Mountsville was specifically fought. Mr. Seaton says, "Look the roads just don't go that way."

"Mountsville is not that big," says Mr. Stuart, "All we have to do is find one of those gun emplacements. It's got to be close."

"There ought to be another way of doing it," says Mr. Craun, "If they're traveling up an Unfrequented Road—they have to drop things on that road. We can pick it up that way."

"Well, who brought that note to General Stuart?" says Mr. Seaton, "We know that they lived at Mountsville. Look here at Yardley Taylor's map. You see at Carters."

"Possibly," says Mr. Craun, "But look at the road, on the map, it doesn't go that way."

"Oh, yes it does," states Mr. Stuart, "It makes that exact T in the road."

"That's not a T," says Mr. Craun, "That's a triangle."

"Ok, let's make an overlay," says Mr. Seaton, "From Yardley Taylor's map to a modern map, which should get us relatively close and get us on the old road."

"You hope so," says Mr. Stuart.

As the evening grew on, the four banshees listened to the description of the battle, the troops involved, and about how to possibly get to this camp. Mrs. Craun and Mrs. Stuart knock on the Unison store door calling for their husbands. "It's 7:00 PM," says Mrs. Craun, "The kids with you?"

Mr. Seaton answers the door, "The kids aren't with us. We thought they were with you."

Mrs. Stuart retorts, "You know we had the bazaar to handle – you've been gone for hours."

Mr. Stuart replies, "Well, where could those kids be?" With that, the four banshees sneak down the stairs, around the back of the store, through Five Oaks, across the field and into the barn.

Mr. Stuart getting a tad worried, "Ok, Ronnie, you go to the camp. Doug, you go to the church. You two go to the house, and I'll go to Five Oaks. Whoever finds them, we'll all meet at Ronnie's house." As the fathers scour the landscape for the four banshees, Mrs. Craun and Mrs. Stuart return to Mrs. Craun's house. As they get out of the car, they hear giggling and laughing coming from the barn.

The four banshees, after being discovered hear Mrs. Craun exclaim, "Where have you been?"

Cody replies, "Here mom, right here."

Mrs. Stuart asks, "Why didn't you tell us you were leaving the bazaar?"

"Oh, mom," retorts Sean, "We're ok."

"Come on Sean and Heather, it's time to go home," says Mrs. Stuart, "When my husband gets here, send him home."

Mrs. Craun beckons Cody and Cubby inside, "Come on in, Cubby, till your dad get's here."

"Can't we camp out tonight," asks Cody.

"Not tonight," replies Mrs. Craun.

"Aw – you promised," cries Cody.

"No, I didn't promise. This is your father's deal. You need to take it up with him – but not tonight. It's been two really big days. It's time everyone got some rest."

In the meantime, the fathers, not finding the children, return to the Craun's house. As they stand outside in front of the house, Mrs. Craun comes out onto the porch. "The kids are here," says Mrs. Craun, "John, Elizabeth says it's time for you to come on home. And Doug, Cubby is in the house. And, oh yeah, you promised those boys a camping trip. It's only a few days to Halloween, so you handle it."

"Ok, ok," says Mr. Craun, "I know, we promised."

Doug says, "You know what would be cool? We could take those kids camping up by the graveyard by the pond..."

"You need to leave those kids alone," says Mr. Stuart.

"It's Halloween, right?" says Mr. Craun, "We can do all kinds of things. Remember what our fathers did to us? We can hide speakers and make recordings."

"What about lights in the pond?" replies Mr. Seaton.

"Ooh, ooh, we can do gas balloons and anchor them down," says Mr. Craun.

"You're fathers really did that to you?" asks Mr. Stuart.

"Oh, yeah," says Mr. Seaton, "Haven't you ever been to Unison for Halloween night?"

"No," says Mr. Stuart.

"Oh – you ought to see this town," says Mr. Seaton, "From witches that fly across the street to cauldrons boiling to ghost popping out of doors to skeletons that sit up in graves and eerie recordings playing all over town – you'd think this place was Salem, MA. This town goes all out."

"No wonder Mrs. Edwards believes in ghosts," says Mr. Stuart, "Your wives find out and there's going to be big trouble. You're going to have these kids really spooked up."

"Oh, it's good for them, it won't hurt them," replies Mr. Craun.

"Ok," says Mr. Stuart, "But you two are on your own."

A-CAMPING-WE-SHALL-GO

(Chapter 5)

During the week, Mr. Craun and Mr. Seaton were busy setting up preparations to scare the wits out of our four confederate banshees. The men put masks with lights in them, and hid them all around the pond and camping area. They buried balloons with fluorescent light sticks anchoring them to the bottom of the pond with weights so that when they pulled a string the lighted balloons floated towards the surface creating an eerie illusion. The pond would look like it was glowing. The men took an air tank and ran a hose into the bottom of the pond to make sure the pond bubbled for the complete effect. Preparing their headless straw horseman, they readied him for his ride through the kid's camp. And just to make sure that the whole effect was complete, they created one skeleton that could be dropped from a tree at a moments notice. The two fathers were now sure that their gags were ready, began to taunt and prep the kids for what they thought would be a magnificent night of adventure. Unexpectedly, that week the weather took a sharp drop in temperature and it looked like the kid's camping trip was going to be cancelled. However, for some reason to the mother's amazement, the fathers were almost insistent that they would be fine.

41

It was a chilly October night, so the father's made a bonfire to help keep the kid's warm and told them to have a good night. They told the kids that they would come back to check on them later. Sean is holding a hot dog over the embers of the fire complaining persistently to his sister, "I don't see why you had to tag along on a boy's camping trip."

"I'm not tagging along. I was invited, and I'm part of this club too," cries Heather, "Besides you need me – I'm not afraid of anything. Who's going to protect you, when the ghosts come out?"

Cody, trying to break up the argument replies, "You know, we are awfully close to the graveyard. Why do we have to camp so close to the graveyard, anyway?"

Cubby adds, "Yeah, it's mighty spooky here." There is an awkward silence as the kid's take in the sounds of the evening.

As the night begins to settle in, the two fathers take their places to begin their haunting. Cody getting a tad bored says, "Why don't we tell some ghost stories."

"That's a great idea, Cody," replies Heather.

"I know a doozy," answers Sean.

"Ok – let's hear it," says Cubby, "I love a good ghost story." Sean starts to tell his story steeped with confederate soldiers and men who have lost limbs and come back from their graves to reclaim their lost body parts.

"You know," says Cody, "as great of a ghost story as you just told – nothing beats what happened to Mr. Seaton up on Seaton's Hill."

"You really believe that there was a ghost in Mr. Seaton's car?" asks Sean.

"There's no such thing as ghosts," answers Heather.

"Well if there's no such thing as ghosts," says Sean, "Why do you run every time we pass the cemetery."

"I don't know," replies Heather, "That place just gives me the creeps. Besides you were running too."

Cubby chimes in, "I need to run to the house."

"All right, go," replies Sean.

"I want someone to go with me," asks Cubby.

"Oh, for goodness sake, Cubby," retorts Sean, "You can see the lights from the barn."

"I'm not going back across that pasture by myself."

"Oh come on Cubby," says Cody, "I'll take you."

"Well, if you're going back," says Sean, "I'm not staying here."

"Well, then you take him back, and I'll stay here," replies Cody.

"Oh for goodness sakes," says Heather, "It's really chilly anyway. Let's all go back and see if Mrs. Craun will make us some hot chocolate." Cubby takes off towards the old farmhouse with the other three at a fast gait behind him. After running a short distance, Cubby trips and falls face down into the dirt. A speaker falls out from the tree next to him landing right by his hand. The fathers now seeing the kids heading back towards the house commence to release their pranks.

With the speakers blaring ghostly haunts, the pond starts to bubble and the lights start to flash. Screeches are heard coming through the trees. The kids stop in their tracks in sheer horror. They look at each other, not knowing what to do. Then, out of a tree pops a skeleton. Heather screams, and Cody grabs her hand. On the other side of the pond, a dense cloud of smoke forms, and as that clears a lit mask appears. With Heather in hand, and not a word said, Cody and the rest of the kids start running up the path toward the barn and corral. When the kids had just about gotten to the gate, a headless horseman appears riding through on a galloping horse. "It's the headless horseman!" cries Cubby, "Run!" The four kids now, at a full gait and screaming, run toward the house.

From the back porch of the house Grandma Craun can be heard hollering, "What is going on out here?" All four kids breathlessly speak at the same time, trying to explain the horrors they had just faced.

Mrs. Craun appears wiping her hands on her apron. She calls across the field, "Ronnie Craun, get in here!" By this time, Mr. Craun and Mr. Seaton had met in the field and are beside themselves with delight at their success with

—

getting a rise out of the four banshees. They make their way back to the house, and commence to taunt the kids about not believing in ghosts.

Mrs. Craun replies, "This is not funny. You scared the kids half out of their wits."

"Will you two ever grow up?" says Grandma Craun, "You kids come on inside this house. This is not appropriate behavior for grown men." Mr. Craun and Mr. Seaton cannot control their laughter.

"Aw, come on," says Mr. Craun, "It's all just in fun."

Mrs. Craun sees a horse out in the pasture, "Is that a horse out of the corral?"

"We'll get it. We'll get it," says Mr. Seaton.

"You'll do more than that. You're going to apologize to these kids and clean up this mess."

"Ok, ok," replies Ronnie, "We'll take care of it." The kids go into the house where Grandma Craun makes them each a cup of hot chocolate. None of them intend to sleep in the camp that night, so they set up sleeping arrangements in the living room, and try their best to watch TV and go to sleep. The fear dissipates as the evening passes, and that fear turns itself into discussions of how to get even with their dads by morning.

LIVE-SHELLS

(Chapter 6)

The next morning, Mrs. Craun ushers the kids out of the house, and asks them to take the horses out for a ride and give them some exercise. The kids are all too happy with this arrangement, and decide to ride over to their camp site from the night before. The kids head first over to where Cubby tripped. They find the speaker lying on the ground. Sean says, "I think we need to see how they did this?" Sean gets off of his horse and follows the wire to a recorder and then locates the other speakers.

Cody notices the pond, "Look, there are balloons floating on top of the pond."

"We've got to do something to get even," replies Sean.

"Why don't we take one of their metal detecting camps," answers Cody.

"They'll never take us with them," says Heather doubtfully.

Sean says, "Oh we're not going to take them with us. We're going to take the camp ourselves."

"Wait a minute," says Heather, "They'll never let us near their metal detecting machines."

"Oh, we'll work it out," replies Sean.

"Well, where are we going to go?" asks Cubby.

"We'll follow them," replies Sean. With that the four banshees ride over to the country store to plan their heist.

The kids tie up their horses in back of the store. Cubby walks in and says, "Hi dad, can we get something to drink?"

"Yeah, go get yourselves some sodas," says Mr. Seaton, "How are my four little chickens this morning?" Mr. Seaton starts to make ghostly noises and then proudly smirks.

"Yeah, yeah, yeah," retorts Sean. "Very funny." The kids grab their sodas, and start to head out the door. Mr. Seaton hears one of the kids talking under their breath, "We'll get even," which makes him laugh to himself.

Mr. Stuart comes up the front steps of the store seeing the kids, "Hey kids, all of you ok?"

Sean answers, "Yeah dad. Going metal detecting?"

"Yes as soon as Mr. Craun and Ms. Connors get here."

"Ok, dad," says Sean, "See you later."

The kids get the horses and Sean says, "Cubby, you stay here and watch which way they go. We'll go back to the barn and wait for you there." Cubby stays around back watching out for the fathers to leave. Cubby slyly rides his horse behind the houses, out in the pasture following the fathers to see where they go. The fathers walk up the road and turn to the right and disappear up the creek bed.

Cubby returns to the barn and announces, "They disappeared up the creek bed."

"Ok," says Cody, "we can take the horses and cut across the pasture. We can tie the horses up at Mrs. Connors, and hit the creek bed that way."

"Now we can't be seen," says Sean.

"We'll just stay out of sight and follow them," replies Cody. The kids quickly get to the gully where the fathers have started to metal detect. They sneak along the tree line until they can observe the fathers clearly in the valley below them.

Mr. Seaton gets a really loud signal off of his metal detector. He takes off his headset and yells, "Listen to this."

Mr. Stuart is also getting a strong signal replies, "You listen. Maybe we've got artillery shells."

"Maybe, be careful," says Mr. Craun, "For goodness sakes don't hit them."

The men dig for about five minutes when Mr. Stuart explains, "Oh, oh, got one!" Mr. Craun and Mr. Seaton take off over to the spot where Mr. Stuart has been digging.

Mr. Seaton cries, "Be careful. It may be live. Be careful."

Mr. Stuart replies, "You want to dig it?"

Mr. Seaton answers, "You found it. You dig it. I've already dug a hole two and a half feet deep for mine."

"Maybe we ought to think about this," says Mr. Craun. In the meantime, the kids, hearing all of the excitement try to move stealthily into a better scouting position. Mr. Craun and Mr. Stuart start to dig a bigger hole to retrieve the target, but Mr. Seaton impatiently returns to his target to see what he has.

Suddenly, a loud voice can be heard over the men's heads, "Oh, oh! It's a live shell! I dropped it!" Doug Seaton comes rolling down the hill, and the two other fathers jump to the ground and flatten themselves out. A large thud echoes throughout the valley. After a few seconds, not hearing a large explosion, the three fathers look up and see the four banshees standing on a rock bluff right above the shell hole.

Mr. Stuart alarmed and shocked yells out, "Heather and Sean, you get out of here right now. You could have been killed!!"

Mr. Seaton shouts out, "Cubby, what are you doing here? Go home. Go home now, and don't ever come back here. You kids stay away from here."

"On second thought," says Mr. Stuart, "You stay right there." The three fathers climb up the hill to where the kids are.

"Look, we know you kids want to go metal detecting," says Mr. Craun, "and we will find a place to take you, but there are live shells all over this place. If we or you hit one – you wouldn't be around to tell the story."

"Oh, dad," says Cody, "You always say that."

"Cubby," says Mr. Seaton, "You kids go home, and don't you ever, ever come back to this valley again. It's too dangerous."

"We have another place, and if it works out," says Mr. Stuart, "We'll take you there. –

———

And don't you dare tell your mothers about this. Now go on home." The four kids belligerently returned to their horses and head for home, while the three fathers continued digging their targets. They carefully placed their time-delay Bormann shell in a bucket of mud and water, and carried it to the store. They dug a hole and filled it with water, mud, and sand to protect it until they could find time to have the shell disarmed.

SHHH! SECRETS!

(Chapter 7)

After secretly dispensing of their artillery shell, the fathers stumble into the old store jubilant over their finds for the day. "One time-delayed Bormann, one solid reed shell, and the bottom of a flag staff," says Mr. Stuart, "What a day."

Mr. Craun replies, "You think the bottom of that flag staff was a color sergeant's?"

"What do you think?" says Mr. Seaton, "The Official Records say that Pelham fired into the valley below striking the color sergeant dead using solid reeds and time delay Bormann's to try to catch them when they crossed the creek. It's got to be. We're finding everything that General Stuart wrote about in the OR's."

"If our wives find out about those artillery shells, and those kids," says Mr. Craun, "We could be in some big trouble."

"Forget the kids," says Mr. Stuart, "If they find out we've been digging live artillery shells we're still in big trouble."

Mr. Craun answers, "Those kids wouldn't tell, would they?"

"I don't think they understood what was really going on," said Mr. Seaton.

"Well, you ran your big mouth and told them not to tell their mothers," insisted Mr. Craun.

"Well, I heard through the grapevine that those kids are pretty upset over someone who pulled some pretty nasty pranks," says Mr. Stuart, "And I don't know much, but I know Sean and Cody are probably looking to get even."

"Oh, they wouldn't do that," says Mr. Seaton.

"I don't know," says Mr. Craun, "I think we just need to make it up to them, and find a place to take them metal detecting."

"Well, that's not as easily said as done," replies Mr. Stuart, "Every place we've found is dug out, and we sure can't take them to where we're digging now. Ok – pull out the OR's, we're just going to have to find another camp to take the kid's to."

"Mountsville," says Mr. Craun, "Let's take them to Mountsville."

"Uh, I don't know," says Mr. Seaton, "They were firing shells there, too."

"Well, it's already cold," said Mr. Stuart, "and the way this year is going the ground will be frozen soon. It could take us months to find another camp. We're bearing down on Mountsville. Let's see if we can find it."

Mr. Seaton answers, "That's really ironic – Mountsville was fought October 31st in the middle of the night."

While the fathers were burying their shells, the four confederate banshees were unsaddling, wiping down, and currying their horses in the barn. Mrs. Craun appears at the fence of the barn, "Have you kids seen your fathers?"

—

Cody slyly looks at his mom, "The last time we saw them, they were metal detecting." Mrs. Craun asks, "You went metal detecting with your fathers?"

"No," says Sean.

"Well, how do you know they went metal detecting."

"Oh, we went riding across the field and saw them," says Cody.

"Well, it's getting close to dinner," says Mrs. Craun, "Are you kids hungry?"

"No thank you Mrs. Craun," replies Heather, "We've got to go home."

"What about you Cubby?"

Cubby replies, "I think my dad's back at the store hiding something they don't want you to know about."

"What are you talking about?" asks Mrs. Craun.

"Aw mom, Cubby doesn't know what he's talking about," answers Cody.

"Oh yes I do," says Cubby.

"Are you sure you kids weren't with your father's metal detecting?"

"No, mom, they ran us away."

"Well, if you kids are going home – why don't you go to the store and hurry your fathers up, so dinner doesn't get cold." With that the four kids run across the field, through Mrs. Connor's back yard and over to the store.

As the kids approach the store, Cody shushes the other kids and sneaks up onto the porch looking quietly through the windows. The fathers are steady at work with their research.

There are maps and books strewn all over the store. Sean signals to the others to be quiet and the four kids scramble up the rear steps of the store to their clubhouse to take their spying positions to see what their fathers were up to. The men looked like soldiers reviewing their battle movements and strategies for the next campaign. They were scouring over their maps and paperwork discussing locations the armies were supposed to have been in, and the people who had lived in the area. It was getting dark, but through the dim light in the store, Mr. Stuart still wearing his Australian hat, could be seen saying, "Carter – where's Carter? There's only one old house left at Mountsville. It's got to be Mrs. Hayne's home."

"They'll never let us on their property," says Mr. Craun.

"Look at the map. Look at the map, "says Mr. Stuart, "Look at the roads at Mountsville. They don't do what they do today."

"Yes, they do," says Mr. Craun.

"No, they don't," says Mr. Seaton, "See the roads going to Pothouse. When I was a kid there was a store on the corner. See the road going at an angle – I wonder if that's the Unfrequented Road?"

"Ok, ok," says Mr. Stuart, "Let's get some paper. Let's trace it out." Diligently, using a ruler, figuring the distance from every point they knew that existed today, the men compared it to the roads on the old map. The fathers began to trace the distances from the bridge on Goose Creek to known intersections and buildings.

"They had to have been in the woods by the creek," says Mr. Seaton.

"Maybe," says Mr. Craun, "but we've got to find where General Stuart set up his artillery."

"Ok, ok," says Mr. Stuart, "In the morning, one of us needs to take a ride over to Mountsville and see what it looks like. I can't, I've got to go to work."

"I've got too much to do tomorrow," says Mr. Craun.

"I'll go," replies Mr. Seaton.

"Oh, yeah, yeah," answers Mr. Craun, "Here we go again. You get there before any of us."

"Oh, for goodness sake," says Mr. Seaton, "I won't take your bloody camp if I find it."

"Yeah, right," retorts both Mr. Craun and Mr. Stuart. Mr. Seaton carefully rolls up their newly traced map and the old tattered army map and places it on a shelf behind the counter. Sean signals to the other kids to quietly exit the clubhouse.

When the kids reach the bottom of the stairs Sean and Cody give a sly look to each other and Sean says to Cody, "Got them!"

"What do you mean got them?" asks Heather.

"We're going to take their camp," answers Cody.

"When?" asks Heather, "It's almost Halloween."

"Halloween." replies Sean.

———

55

"Oh, no," says Cubby, "I'm going trick-or-treating."

"You'll go trick-or-treating," says Sean, "We'll get the camp after we've gone trick-or-treating."

"It'll be dark," replies Heather.

Cubby says curtly, "You're not going."

"Oh, yes I am," retorts Heather.

"Well, we don't even know where we're going or how we're going to get there yet." With that the three fathers can be heard coming out of the door of the store, so Cody signals to the rest to follow him.

"Dad," says Cody, "Mom says it's time to come home and dinner's ready."

"Ok, Cody," says Mr. Craun, "We're coming."

Mr. Seaton gestures to Cubby, "Come on, Cubby, get in the car. We're going home." Mr. Stuart opens the door to his truck and signals to Heather and Sean to get in.

As they are about to leave Mr. Craun rolls down the window of his car and says, "I will come by here tomorrow, your metal detector better still be in the store."

"Ok, ok," says Mr. Seaton, "I think all machines should be left in the store."

"Well, that will stop everyone from going metal detecting without the other." Mr. Seaton gets out of his car, opens the door of the store, and signals for the other two to stack their metal detectors in the back corner of the store. Sean and Cody look at each other, not believing in

———

their good fortune. The three vehicles pull out of the store driveway and head home.

THE SECRET PLAN

(Chapter 8)

Mr. Stuart and his children get home and find Mrs. Stuart in the kitchen preparing dinner. Looking up from the stove, Mrs. Stuart asks, "Where have you all been?"

"Oh, we went metal detecting for a while."

"Uh-huh, and what did you find?"

"Oh, just the bottom of a flag staff pole."

"They found more than that," says Sean.

Mr. Stuart gives a sharp look at Sean, "How do you know?"

"Mom," Heather breaks in. "What are we having for dinner?"

"I talked to Mrs. Craun," says Mrs. Stuart ignoring Heather's question, "What have you been up to?"

"Don't worry," says Mr. Stuart, "We just found a few shell fragments."

"John, what have I told you about taking those kids metal detecting?" says Mrs. Stuart.

"Oh, they didn't take us metal detecting," replies Heather.

"Well, what were you all doing?" Mrs. Stuart asks Heather and Sean.

"We just went horseback riding," says Heather.

"They were just close by," says Mr. Stuart.

"While you were digging shells?" asks Mrs. Stuart.

"Oh, they weren't that close, and they were just shell fragments," answered Mr. Stuart hoping not to get caught, "and they weren't whole shells anyway." Sean and Heather look at each other sheepishly and try to change the subject.

"Mom," cries Sean, "What are we having for dinner?"

Mrs. Stuart says, "You kids get washed up and sit down at the table. Dinner will be ready in a few minutes."

"I think I'll go get cleaned up, too," says Mr. Stuart.

"This conversation's not over, John," replies Mrs. Stuart.

"Ok, ok honey," says Mr. Stuart as he quickly exits the room.

The next morning the mothers greet each other on the lawn of Unison Church. Mrs. Craun says to Mrs. Stuart, "Did you find out what the guys are up to?"

"I think they're digging artillery shells," replies Mrs. Stuart.

"Ronnie didn't say anything about it," says Mrs. Craun, "He couldn't possibly keep quiet about something like that."

"Doug was beside himself last night," says Mrs. Seaton, "They found something."

"Somehow these kids are involved in this," worries Mrs. Stuart.

"Ronnie would never let those kids get near any danger," says Mrs. Craun.

"I'm telling you," says Mrs. Stuart, "they're up to something. We better keep our eyes open. You know how they are about Civil War artifacts. You don't think they're digging live artillery shells do you?"

"I sure hope not," says Mrs. Seaton, "knowing those three, all three of us or one of us could end up a widow."

"I think we all better go in and say a good prayer," jokes Mrs. Craun.

The four confederate banshees had slipped around the corner of the church, and huddled together for a private conversation. "We need to get that map," says Cody.

"The store's closed today," says Cubby.

Sean says, "We need to get the key."

"Wait, Dad will open for a little bit," answers Cubby, "I will pull the wood latch out of the attic door from upstairs."

"Ok, ok," says Sean, "What do we tell our moms?"

"I think the horses should be exercised today," says Cody.

"I'd like to go riding any way," says Heather. With that the church bell can be heard ringing, and the preacher is encouraging his parishioners to come into the church. The kids scurry into church waiting for their next adventure.

When church was finally over and they were able to get a chance to ask, the kids request to go horseback riding. "You just went riding yesterday," says, Mrs. Stuart. "Mrs.

Craun doesn't need to be watching you 24 hours a day."

"I don't mind," says Mrs. Craun, "I enjoy having them."

"Where are you kids going?" asks Mrs. Seaton.

"Just around," says Cody.

"You're not going where you were yesterday, are you?" asks Mrs. Stuart.

"Oh, mom," says Sean.

"Can't we just ride around the back pasture?" asks Heather.

"Ok," says Mrs. Stuart, "But don't you leave the Craun property."

"Well, that's not very far," retorts Cubby.

Cody gives a stern look to Cubby. "It's ok - we'll just ride around the farm."

"You're coming home for lunch," says Mrs. Stuart to Sean and Heather. "Your grandmother's coming from town."

Cody and Sean take Cubby aside, "Ok, ok – remember what you're supposed to do, right?"

"No problem," says Cubby, "Dad always stops at the store anyway."

"Don't you get caught!" warns Cody.

"I'll be quiet as a mouse," says Cubby.

"Oh, yeah," jokes Sean, "That'll be the day."

At 2:00 PM the kids meet back at the Craun farm in the barn. "How did you do, Cubby?" asks Sean, "How did you do?"

"Piece of cake," replies Cubby.

"Ok – let's ride the horses to the back of the farm and tie them up," says Cody. "Then we can go across the church, through the old baseball field, and cross the road to the store." The four kids successfully reach their clubhouse and pull the hatch to enter from the attic down the steps into the store. Cody quickly goes to the back of the counter and removes the old tattered army map and studies the overlay the fathers have made.

"Boy," Sean says, "This is quite a ways. How are we going to get there? It's too far to walk."

"We can ride our horses," says Cody.

"It's going to be dark," says Heather.

"Ok, we'll ride up the old road by our house," says Sean, "and go across Turkey Roost."

"We're going to have to hook up lights to the horses," says Cody, "Each of us needs to get a shovel and a flash light. We've got to be back by 9:00 pm."

"How are we going to get the horses out of the paddock?" asks Heather.

"We just have to be careful," says Sean, "They ought to be so busy trying to scare the other kids. We might be able to get away with it."

"Our mothers won't be busy," replies Heather.

"Well, they've got the party at the church, right?" asks Cody, "Cubby wants to go trick-or-treating - so you two take Cubby and I'll get the horses ready. We'll all meet at the barn at 6:00 PM. We can be there, do an hour of hunting, and be back before they know what happened." Cody starts to make a sketch of his father's map, when the kids hear the rumbling of a car pulling up in front of the store.

Cubby bolts to the window to see what is going on outside, "Oh, oh. It's dad! It's dad!" Cody whispers. "Put the map away put the map away." Sean grabs the map to put it away, but can't remember where it went. He leaves it on the counter, as the four confederate banshees scramble up the pull down stairs, and then pull the stairs up to close them. Mr. Seaton enters the store and goes behind the counter to get his accounting books. The four kids being beside themselves with excitement and glee start to giggle.

Cody whispers, "Shh—be quiet." Cubby is laughing so hard he is totally losing his composure and lands with his hand in the middle of a doll stored in the attic.

"Whaa..." cries the doll. All four kids freeze looking at each other for what to do. Mr. Seaton, not quite sure of what he is hearing, thoroughly looks over the store – looking in every nook and cranny, "That doggone ghost just won't leave me alone!" Sean is hyperventilating – trying to control himself from laughing out loud. Sean watches Mr. Seaton go back to retrieving the books and sees Mr. Seaton notice that his map has moved.

"Oh – I know I didn't put that map there," says Mr. Seaton to himself. Mr. Seaton's imagination is now in full gear. Looking around in the store, every sound now begins to drive his imagination more. Speaking in a loud voice to no one Mr. Seaton retorts, "Ok, ok, I don't know who you are. I don't know what you want, but I'm still going metal detecting!" With that he hurriedly leaves the store, and heads to Mr. Craun for moral support. The four kids bust out laughing, and sneak back down to the store to quickly finish sketching their map. With that the kids head back to retrieve their horses.

When the kids arrive back at the barn, they find Mr. Craun working on the tractor with Mr. Seaton standing over him retelling his story about the ghost.

Mr. Craun slides out from underneath the tractor and starts to laugh, "Doug Seaton, there are no such things as ghosts. You need to get a hold of yourself."

"I'm telling you," says Mr. Seaton, "I'm telling you – a baby cried in the store." Hearing this, it is everything the kids can do to keep their composure.

Mrs. Craun calls out from the house porch, "Brush those horses down good, kids. Cubby, your mom is coming to get you and I have cookies and hot chocolate for you if you want it." The kids finish their chore and head towards the house for their treat. When they enter, they find Grandma Craun, Mrs. Craun and Mrs. Seaton milling through old trunks of clothes.

—

"Mom," says Mrs. Craun, "I don't know what to make for a Halloween costume this year."

Mrs. Seaton looks at Cubby and asks, "Cubby, what do you want to be for Halloween?"

"I want to wear my uniform," replies Cubby.

"Well, I want to wear my uniform," says Sean.

"What about you, Heather, what do you want to be?" asks Mrs. Craun.

"I don't know," replies Heather.

"Well, would you like to wear my great grandmother's dress?" asks Mrs. Craun.

"Can I?" asks Heather.

"Ok, that's cool," replies Cody. "We can all go trick-or-treating together dressed as confederates."

Mrs. Craun exclaims to Mrs. Seaton, "Oh, thank goodness. I don't have to worry about Halloween costumes this year." With that the kids finished their hot chocolate and cookies and cakes.

Mr. Craun enters seeing Mrs. Seaton and exclaims, "You're husband is at it again. His ghosts are now visiting him at the store."

Mr. Seaton entering right behind him retorts back, "I'm telling yah. There's a baby crying in the store." The four kids dash out of the house and begin laughing hysterically around the corner.

Sean tells Heather, "I think we'd better go home."

"Cubby you make sure you get that attic door latched," warns Cody. "Wait, wait, thinks Cody. we still have to get the machines. Can you get the latch so that it looks like it's locked?"

Cubby thinks for a second, "I'll just partially slide the wood into the latch, so we can vibrate the wood and get it to fall out."

"Are you sure?" asks Sean. "I'll figure out something," says Cubby. Their long adventurous weekend was finally over, and the kids went to their respective homes and dragged through their long week of school. They couldn't wait to go on their Halloween adventure, and every chance they could get the next week, they would try to plan and talk about it.

HISTORY, OH YES, HISTORY

(Chapter 9)

Mr. Seaton had asked Mrs. Connors to watch the store for him on Tuesday morning. Picking up his maps and his books, he travels to Mountsville. He carefully reviews his maps and checks the distance between Goose Creek Bridge, the Carter House, and what he believes is the old store. He begins to notice a trench in the ground running across the pastures. He reviews the maps and begins thinking to himself, "That has got to be the old road." He gets out of his car and scurries up the trenched ground until he reaches the woods above the creek. Traveling through the woods, he reaches an embankment overlooking the road. To his amazement, he finds two places where the ground had been dug out to put artillery. "Oh, oh, got you," says Mr. Seaton. He scrambles back to his car and quickly returns to his store exuberant with delight over his new find. Not being able to keep it to himself, he picks up the phone and calls Mr. Craun. "Ronnie," says Mr. Seaton, "You're not going to believe it, but I found them."

"What did you find?" asks Mr. Craun.

"The old road," replies Mr. Seaton, "And two artillery rudouts."

"Two artillery rudouts?" questions Mr. Craun. "Where?"

"Above Goose Creek," replies Mr. Seaton, "In the woods. Just above the banks of the road. Want to go hunting?"

"I can't," says Mr. Craun, "I've got to help dad bring in the corn."

"Aw, come on Ronnie," taunts Mr. Seaton.

"I can't," Mr. Craun explains, "and don't you dare go without me. Besides, we promised John we wouldn't go without him."

"I'm sure I've got it," says Mr. Seaton, "I'm sure I've got it."

"Yeah, you've been sure a hundred times before and didn't have it. Why don't I call John, and we all meet at the store to review what you've got."

Mr. Seaton agrees. "Ok, Mrs. Connors can only watch the store today – Call John and we'll all get together Wednesday night."

"You know, we have to get ready for Halloween, too," reminds Mr. Craun.

"Aw, geez," says Mr. Seaton, "How are we going to do all of this?"

"Mountsville has been there 150 years," says Mr. Craun, "It will still be there weekend after next. And we still have to take John to Seaton's Hill."

Wednesday evening the store is bustling with activity. The three old men are huddled around the wood stove playing checkers, having no intention of leaving into the cold night air. At about 6:30 pm Mr. Craun and Mr. Stuart arrive at the store finding Mr. Seaton full of delight from his research of the past few days. "Mr. Carter,", asks Mr. Seaton, "Do you know where your relatives lived?"

"Sure," says Mr. Carter.

"Anyone live at Mountsville?"

"No, not that I know of," replies Mr. Carter, "I had some up at Aldie. His house was a hospital."

"Oh, yeah," said Mr. Delaney, "His great uncle lived there."

"But nobody at Mountsville," asks Mr. Craun.

"No," replies Old Man Carter. Josh answers, "There was an old road outside of Middleburg that ran to Aldie that Mosby used." With that the three old men began to argue over the Civil War and things that they thought they knew.

"Ok," cuts in Mr. Seaton, "I've got to close the store." The old men give Mr. Seaton a look, pick up their canes, and Mr. Seaton scurries the rest of his customers outside the door.

Mr. Seaton locks the door and speaks to his two comrades, "I've got them. I've got them."

"Got what?," asks Mr. Stuart.

"Mountsville," says Mr. Seaton, "I found them at Mountsville."

"Found what?" asks Mr. Stuart.

"He thinks he's got two artillery sites," answers Mr. Craun.

"You been metal detecting," worries Mr. Stuart.

"No, no, no – no one went metal detecting without you," answers Mr. Seaton, "I just went on a scouting mission."

"And you found two artillery rudouts?" asks Mr. Stuart.

"Yes, I found two artillery sites," replies Mr. Seaton, "I'm sure of it."

"Yeah, yeah, yeah," replies Mr. Craun. "You've had us scrambling over hill and dale for things you've said you've found. We've never been this lucky to find it this fast." Mr. Seaton grabs his maps and books, throws it over the counter, and retorts, "Well, this time I've found them. Look at the maps." With that Mr. Stuart, Mr. Craun, and Mr. Seaton review the overlay map that they had made, which Mr. Seaton has marked up.

"Ok, ok," says Mr. Stuart, "I think we need to review the Official Records to see what they have to say. My memory is not that good." Mr. Seaton opens the OR and turns to the Union/Bloomfield section and starts to review what General Stuart has to say about Mountsville. Mr. Seaton begins to read,

No. 11

Report of Maj. Gen. J. E. B. Stuart, C. S. Army commanding cavalry, of operations
October 30- November 6
HDQRS. CAVALRY CORPS, ARMY OF NORTHERN VIRGINIA,

February 27, 1864.

On October 30, 1862, it having been ascertained that the enemy had crossed the Potomac in force in the vicinity of Leesburg, I was directed by the commanding general to cross at once with the brigade of my command into Loudoun, with a view to watch the enemy's movements... I crossed with Fitz Lee's brigade, under Col. Williams C. Wickman (Brig. Gen. Fitz. Lee having been disabled), and six pieces of the Stuart Horse Artillery, under Maj. John Pelham, at Castleman's Ferry and Snicker's Gap... Proceeding in the direction of Middleburg I bivouacked near Bloomfield.

Having ascertained during the night that there was a force of the enemy at Mountville where the SnickersvilleTurnpike crosses Goose Creek, I started on the morning of the 31ˢᵗ with the command for that point. Pursuing an unfrequented road, I succeeded in surpassing the enemy, who were in force of about 100, and dispersing the whole without difficulty; killed and captured nearly the whole number, among the former Captain Gove of the First Rhode Island Cavalry

"Ok, ok," says Mr. Stuart, "I don't remember any road."

"It's not a road anymore," says Mr. Seaton. "There's barely any trace of it – just a dent in the ground."

"I don't remember the old store," adds Mr. Craun.

"I remember it from when I was a kid," says Mr. Seaton, "It's still there covered in vines and underbrush."

...The attack was made by the Ninth Virginia in advance, support by the Third, which last continued the pursuit of the fugitives several miles to Aldie. Here, the enemy being in force, the Third Virginia retired to the hill overlooking the town until re-enforced by the rest of the command. The Fourth Virginia, now in advance, pushed on toward the village, meeting midway a column of the enemy charging up the lane...

It was subsequently ascertained that General Bayard was in command of the enemy's forces, and that they retreated, without halting, to Fairfax Court House, and that the reported advance from Mountsville was a mistake. The enemy suffered heavily in killed and wounded.

Our own loss was very slight. In the camp captured at Mountsville, several flags, numbers of saddles, valises, blankets, oil-clothes, and other valuable articles were captured, which the enemy had abandoned in their hasty flight.

"Well, if you found the artillery site," says Mr. Stuart. "We still don't have the Rhode Island camp."

"We just read the ORs," says Mr. Craun, "General Stuart said they went up an Unfrequented Road, set up their artillery, and opened up on the Rhode Island Camp. There's only one way he can be firing, and that's in the woods across the road. That would be behind the Carter house."

"You think it's the Carter House?" says Mr. Stuart.

"It's got to be the Carter house," says Mr. Seaton.

"I don't know. I don't know if that house is old enough," says Mr. Craun.

"Besides, if they were firing across the road," says Mr. Stuart, "It's really a short distance for artillery to be firing."

"They could have been way back in the woods," answers Mr. Seaton.

—

"Picket posts aren't set that far away from the road," says Mr. Stuart, "They would have to have been watching that bridge."

"Well, it's irrelevant," says Mr. Craun. "The only way we're going to know is to go check it out. It all looks pretty good."

"Well, maybe we can go next Sunday," says Mr. Stuart.

"Um – I think we need to take you some place you haven't been to yet," says Mr. Craun.

"What do you mean – someplace I haven't been to yet," asks Mr. Stuart.

"It's a surprise," says Mr. Craun. "And I think you'll be pleasantly surprised."

"Well, why don't you just tell me where we're going," asks Mr. Stuart.

"No, no," says Mr. Craun. "You just wait until Sunday morning."

"I think we need to go to Mountsville," says Mr. Seaton.

"We don't even know that we've got it," says Mr. Craun. "Better to have a bird in the hand than one that can fly away."

"You know it's pretty ironic, Mountsville was fought on October 31st," says Mr. Seaton.

"Oh, so you want to go metal detecting Halloween night at a battlefield?" says Mr. Craun, "Don't you have enough ghosts already?"

"Oh – I think it might be a good idea to wait a couple of weeks," replies Mr. Seaton.

"Besides we've got to get our Halloween stuff ready for the kids on Saturday," says Mr. Craun. "You going to leave the store open for Halloween?"

"Well, it's not going to be open for business," replies Mr. Seaton. "But it's going to be open."

"John, you going to help us get ready for Halloween?" asks Mr. Craun, "We're going to scare the living wits out of these kids."

"Uh – no," answers Mr. Stuart, "that's your thing to do. I'm just going to be an innocent bystander. I don't think you two should be trying to scare little kids."

"Aw come on," answers Mr. Craun, "It's all just in fun."

"Yeah, giving nightmares to four and five years old," says Mr. Stuart, - "great fun."

"They're not all four and five year olds," replies Mr. Seaton. "Our dad's did it to us."

"That doesn't make it right," answers Mr. Stuart.

"Speaking of ghosts, Doug," asks Mr. Craun, "Had any visitors the last couple of days?"

"No," retorts Mr. Seaton.

"What's going on now?" asks Mr. Stuart.

"Not much," says Mr. Craun, "Doug's ghost is living with him in the store now."

"What are you talking about?" asks Mr. Stuart.

"I'm telling you," says Mr. Seaton, "I don't care what you say – there was a baby crying in this store."

"Oh, Doug," retorts Mr. Stuart, "Will you cut out the ghost talk. There is no such thing as ghosts."

"I don't care what you say," answers Mr. Seaton, "I don't care what you do. I tell you, there is a ghost following me around."

"Well, I've got to go home," says Mr. Craun.

"I've got to go home, too," says Mr. Stuart. "We'll just leave you here with your ghost."

"Well, if you're leaving," says Mr. Seaton, "I'm leaving, too. I'm not staying here by myself at night. Not here, not anymore." With that, Mr. Craun and Mr. Stuart begin to laugh, and the three fathers go to their respective homes.

UNISON HALLOWEEN SPOOKS AND GOBLINS

(Chapter 10)

Saturday morning, the residents of Unison are busy readying their town for the evening's festivities. Cauldrons are placed by the side of the road with dry ice and water to produce an eerie smoke. The parents dress up as witches and goblins to greet their trick-or-treaters. Mr. Seaton has rigged up his pulley system in the store for his flying ghost, placing witches and cauldrons on the porch of the store and hiding his record player of eerie sounds. All day long, Mr. Craun and Mr. Seaton scurry up and down the trees, stringing ropes and pulleys for flying ghosts and goblins. They hide their lights and timers to make sure that they are lit at the proper time. They place recorders and speakers all up and down the town to greet the children as they trick-or-treat through town. While this was going on, Mrs. Craun begins to prepare the four confederate banshees for what she believes will be a night of trick-or-treating.

The children are very excited for their adventure. Heather secretly puts her jeans on underneath her hoop skirt, so she will be more easily able to ride her horse. Sean and Heather were able to get flashlights very easily, but had to skillfully get the shovel into the back of the car in order to prevent detection from Mrs. Stuart. Heather and Sean meet Cody and Cubby at the barn as planned. They all say good evening to Mrs. Craun and pretend to head to town. They sneak behind the barn and Cody says, "All right, I'll stay here and get the horses ready. You got your flashlights and shovels? I'll put them in the saddle bags." The kids hand over the equipment.

Cody asks, "Cubby – you got that latch ready?"

"Yeah, it should be fine," replies Cubby.

"Ok, you need to go to the store to get the metal detectors," replies Cody.

"Cubby, we'll go up in the top of the store and go down and get the metal detectors," says Sean. "You keep your father busy."

Cubby, Sean, and Heather head to town to go trick-or-treating, and to get the metal detectors. They stop by the country store and find Mr. Seaton still busily setting up his Halloween display on the front porch of the store. Mr. Seaton looks up to see three young confederates standing in front of him. "Oh, you kids are going to be confederate soldiers for Halloween?" asks Mr. Seaton.

"No one would let me have a uniform," retorts Heather.

"Well, Heather, there were plenty of women who traveled with the Confederate Army. You're just dressed for the time," says Mr. Seaton.

"What're you doing dad?" asks Cubby.

"What does it look like? I'm getting ready for Halloween, Cubby," says Mr. Seaton.

"Can I help?" asks Cubby.

"Sure," replies Mr. Seaton, "Why don't you go inside and get my other witch." Cubby darts in the store – flies to the back store room and pulls the latch on the attic stairs. He returns, picks up the witch and darts over to his father to occupy him while Heather and Sean sneak around the corner and up the stairs to the attic. Sean puts down the pull-down stairs quietly and carefully moves down the stairs and grabs one of the metal detectors from behind the counter. Mr. Seaton takes his extension cord and starts to open the front door so that he can plug in one of his speakers.

Sean quickly ducks, as Cubby yells, "Dad!" Cubby steps backward tripping over the witches cauldron which goes flying into the record player.

"Cubby, are you ok?" asks Mr. Seaton.

"Yeah, dad," replies Cubby. Sean seeing his chance, quickly grabs a metal detector and hands it to Heather who pulls it up into the attic.

He hears Mr. Seaton tell Cubby, "Cubby, why don't you play while I get this set up." Sean gestures to Cubby to keep his dad busy.

"Dad, what is the witch going to do?" asks Cubby. Sean heaves a sigh of relief and grabs the other two metal detectors to hand up to Heather. Mr. Seaton who is very proud of his creation is all too happy to tell Cubby about it. Once they have completed their mission, Sean and Heather peak around the corner and signal to Cubby that they finished. Cubby breaks into his dad's speech and says, "Well, I got to go, Dad. Gotta go."

"Cubby," says Mr. Seaton, "I thought you wanted to know what I was going to do?"

"Aw, gee, dad," replies Cubby, "I'm going to see it soon."

As he darts around the corner of the store, Mr. Seaton shakes his head and says, "Kids."

The kids carefully move through the old baseball field, through the woods, cross the field in front of the church, and pass behind the parsonage to hide their machines at the edge of the woods belonging to Five Oaks. They then proceed to go trick-or-treating for Cubby. They join the rest of the children now beginning to congregate in the street. The three mothers have all met at the church to prepare for the Halloween party. Mr. Craun is at home to greet the trick-or-treaters and has his doormat set up so when it is stepped upon, a speaker blare a ghastly ghost sound. He flies the door open, with the house pitch black, dressed in a bloody logger costume with a hatchet buried in his forehead. Pulling a switch, he has a light underneath his shirt that puts a spotlight on his bloody face. Over at the store, Mr. Seaton, is now waiting for his trick-or-treaters with animated witches, flying ghosts and eerie sounds. He keeps his eyes open to watch for kids who pass by his secret places. He then darts to his hiding place to release his pulley system for his witch to fly across the street or his stuffed-straw dummy to fall from the tree with a hangman's noose on it. It is hard to believe, but Unison took more of a resemblance to Salem Massachusetts than a small southern Virginia country town. People would come for miles just to see the sights and festivities of Unison on Halloween night.

After trick-or-treating, Heather, Sean and Cubby go to the church to strategically check in with their moms. Cubby grabs his share of candy and loot, and the kids sneak across the back of Five Oaks grabbing their metal detectors, and crossing the Craun's pasture to the barn to meet Cody. Cody replies, "Where have you been? It's 6:30. It's getting late. Is everything ok?"

"Yeah, yeah," says Sean, "It just took longer than we thought." The kids quietly walk their horses out the gate, crossing the road, and far into the pasture where they can't be seen. Mounting their horses, they flip on their lights so the horses can see the way, and they began their long journey across the Beaver's pasture, up the unused road by Sean and Heather's house, across the back of Farmer's Delight to Turkey Roost.

—

A LONG JOURNEY'S NIGHT BACK IN TIME

(Chapter 11)

As the kids plod along across the fields, the cold night air begins to take a sharp bite on our four confederate banshees. Heavy dew and fog rises from the ground making it difficult to see where they were going. The moon only being half full gives an eerie glow down onto the four children. The kids have the appearance of confederate raiders of a hundred years ago. Passing through streams and into woodlands, the confederate banshees became silent - no longer quite so sure that the adventure that they had taken on for themselves was wise. "I'm cold," complains Heather.

"I'm scared," replies Cubby.

"We can go back," answers Sean.

"We're almost there," says Cody. "Why should we quit now."

"I can hardly see," says Sean.

"Why don't we turn the lights off on the horses," says Cody. "And let our eyes adjust to the moonlight." Spurring their horses on, they commenced to travel along side of Beaver Dam Creek heading towards Goose Creek when an eerie light appears at the top of a tall bank off in the distance above Beaver Dam Creek.

"What's that?" asks Sean. Cody pulls his horse up, and the others stop beside him, "I don't know."

"Maybe it's a house," says Heather.

—

"That's no house," replies Cody. "Maybe a farmer is burning trash," says Sean.

"Ok, well let's stay on the creek bed," says Cody, "We don't want to be seen."

The kids travel up the creek bed, but before entering the fields of Mountsville the children hear a loud command, "Halt! Who goes there?" Pulling up their horses in great disbelief, the kids see scampering out of the trees, four Union soldiers. They approach the children and stand in front of the horses. One of the Union soldiers grabs the reins of Cody's horse. The other three soldiers have muskets pointed at our four confederate banshees.

"Oh no," retorts Cody, "This is impossible."

"Oh no it's not," retorts the corporal officer of the picket. "Look what we have here, four confederate prisoners trying to get through our picket line."

"This isn't funny, guys," says Heather, "You're scaring us."

"You should be scared," answers the corporal, "There's no more war for you."

"Aw, come on guys," says Sean, "Are you trick-or-treating, too?"

"Trick or treating?" says one of the other soldiers. "Maybe you thought you were going to trick us, but you didn't get by us. You're our prisoners now."

"There's something wrong here," says Sean.

"The only thing wrong," answers the corporal, "is you got caught and you're our prisoners. Dismount! Get off those horses." The kids quickly get off the horses. Cody grabs Heather's hand and places himself in front of her.

"Where are your weapons?" asks the Corporal.

"We don't have any weapons," replies Cody.

"Look at this one." says another soldier, "They're really picking them young now. This one's barely ten years old and down to using females, too."

"We aren't soldiers," says Sean, "and this is impossible."

"It might be impossible to you," says the Corporal, "but if you're not soldiers you shouldn't be wearing these uniforms. Ok no more talking." The Corporal yells in a loud piercing voice. "Sergeant of the guard, Sergeant of the guard!" Within a few moments, cantering out of the mist, on the field Sergeant O'Grady arrives on his large black stallion. Sergeant O'Grady was a rough Irishman with fiery red hair and beard. His rough demeanor and presence of command petrified his own men let alone the kids who were now quivering in front of him.

The Sergeant appearing through the night, sees the four young confederates and says, "They're only kids."

"That's what we've been trying to tell you," says Sean, "We're only kids."

85

"Well, you might be young," retorts Sergeant O'Grady, "But those uniforms fit you to a T. And we have some – just as young as you. Corporal, escort your prisoners back to camp. There will be no talking or communications in the ranks. Stay in single file and keep your mouths shut." In total disbelief and astonishment, shaking in their boots, the four young children were led off to the main camp.

When the kids arrive at the camp, Sergeant O'Grady was standing by a large fire in the center having a conversation with Lieutenant Harris. Lieutenant Harris was a dashing, tall, dark-haired twenty-eight year-old from the state of Rhode Island.

The kids hear Sergeant O'Grady whispering to the Lieutenant, "They're just kids. They have no weapons, and something seems out of place here."

"Well, they might be just kids. I don't know what's going on, but we can't take any chances," replies the Lieutenant, "We'll put their horses in the paddock, and bring them over to the fire where we can keep them warm and interrogate them." The kids stare in disbelief at the Union camp and all the sights and sounds that were somewhat familiar to them from their experience with Unison Day a couple of weeks beforehand.

86

UNBELIEVABLE, GREAT DISCOVERIES

(Chapter 12)

As the four banshees walk into the light of the campfire, Lieutenant Harris retorts, "Oh my God. They're only kids!"

"I told you," says the Sergeant.

"Yeah," answers the Lieutenant in disbelief, "But their only kids!"

"They've got Confederate artillery buttons on their uniforms," says the Sergeant.

"These kids can't be artillerists," replies the Lieutenant.

"I don't know," says the Sergeant. "Something's not right."

"And for them to be artillerists," says the Lieutenant, "There would have to be a main army around us. Sergeant, you'd better double the picket guard."

"Corporal Keaty, bring those prisoners here", says the Lieutenant. As the kids draw closer he asks, "What unit are you all with?"

"We're not with any unit," answers Cody.

"Where were you going?" asks the Lieutenant.

"I think we were coming here," answers Cody.

"Aha," says the Sergeant, "You knew we were here."

"Yes and no," answers Sean.

"What do you mean yes and no?" asks the Lieutenant.

"Well not today," answers Cody, "But a hundred years ago."

Corporal Keaty approaches the campfire with the three metal detectors in hand, "Lieutenant, look at these weapons."

"They're not weapons," replies Cody.

"That's the most unusual looking thing I've ever seen," replies the Lieutenant, "What are these?"

"Metal detectors," answers Cubby.

"Metal detectors?" asks the Lieutenant very curious, "What do you mean metal detectors? What kind of metal are you looking for, iron, gold, and silver?"

"Well, you could," Cody answers, "But they're not very good for that."

The Sergeant huffs, "They're weapons."

"They're used for finding artifacts," says Cody.

"What artifacts?" asks the Lieutenant.

"You know, like bullets and buttons," says Cody. "Like the buttons on your uniform."

"Uh-huh," pipes in the Sergeant. "So you use it for finding us."

"No," says Sean. "We use it for finding your buttons a hundred years from now."

"Oh, so how do these metal detectors work?" asks the Lieutenant.

"Off of batteries," answers Sean.

"Oh, no," answers the Sergeant, "I know those aren't batteries. Batteries are big - it takes a whole wagon to hold a battery."

—

"Not anymore," says Heather.

Corporal Keaty says, "Sergeant, you better take a look at this."

"Now I know this is a weapon," says the Sergeant as he holds up a flashlight.

"It's a flashlight," replies Heather.

"A what light?" asks the Lieutenant.

"A flashlight," answers Sean. "It runs off of batteries."

"There you go with that battery talk again," retorts the Sergeant. "Don't you go there again."

"Look," says Cody. "Let me show you how it works."

The corporal lowers his bayonet into Cody's stomach and says, "Don't move."

"Look it's just a flashlight," says Heather, "Let me show you, or push the button on top."

The Lieutenant looks at the Sergeant, "Don't you push that button."

"It just makes light!" shouts Sean getting frustrated. With that, the Lieutenant looks at the flashlight, pointing the large head at Cody, and presses the button. He is astonished when the flashlight comes on to reveal Cody in a bright light as the fire would give.

"Son of a gun," says the Sergeant, "How does this thing work?"

All four of the kids say together, "Batteries!"

"Ok, ok," reflects the Lieutenant. "Let me think. Where are you kids from?"

"Unison," says Cody.

Heather whispers to Cody, "Union."

—

The Lieutenant not noticing and in total disbelief asks, "Where's Unison?"

"Oh, oh yeah," answers Cody, "a hundred years ago it was Union."

"All right - you're trying to tell us now, that you're from a hundred years from now," says the Sergeant. "That you're looking for us, that you have a machine that finds metal, that you have a light that operates off of batteries, and you expect us to believe you."

"Well, technically," says Sean, "We didn't really want to find you. We just wanted to find what you left behind."

"Man, we sure didn't want to find you," says Cubby.

As this conversation has been developing the camp of soldiers have all come to hear and see the spectacle taking place in front of the fire.

"This is crazy - take these kids down to the mill and put a guard on them, and you men get back to your duties," commands the Lieutenant. Two guards escort the kids down to a mill, which is a quarter of a mile down Goose Creek.

The Lieutenant was speaking to the Sergeant as he turns the flashlight on and off, "Look at this. Sergeant, what do you think?"

"I think we've lost the war," answers the Sergeant.

"I don't know," says Corporal Keaty, "The Rebs can't be this advanced."

"No, nobody has this kind of stuff," thinks the Lieutenant.

———

"You think they're telling the truth?" asks the Sergeant.

"I don't know what to think," answers the Lieutenant, "When the captain gets back we'll dump it in his lap. In the meantime, Tommy and Johnny are about their age, right?"

"Well, yeah," answers the Sergeant.

"All right, have them go down to the mill," says the Lieutenant, and befriend those kids and see what they can find out. Get a couple of men to start a fire and bring them blankets to get them warmed up, but keep the rest of the men away from them. Maybe if we can get them settled down, we can make some sense out of this."

"Lieutenant," asks the Sergeant, "What's an artifact?"

"Things that are very old, Sergeant," says the Lieutenant, "like in Roman times."

"Are they trying to say we're artifacts?" asks the Sergeant.

"Well, Sergeant," replies the Lieutenant, "In a way, I guess we are. Sergeant, bring Tommy our drummer boy and Johnny the bugler to me. Corporal Keaty, go get those horses and bring them to me."

"Sir," says Sergeant O'Grady," Private Miller and Swan are here."

"Tommy," says the Lieutenant, "I want you and Johnny to go down to the mill, and I want you to make friends with the four young confederates we found in the woods. I want you to find out everything you can. Get them to talk as much as you can. I want you to take food and anything that you think will help you find out as much information as you can get from them, and don't you forget that they are our enemy." Private Keaty arrives with the horses at this point.

The Lieutenant replies, "Tommy, wait a minute. What is on these horses?"

"I don't know," answers Private Keaty, "but these are the most unusual shovels I have ever seen. Look, it opens up and closes."

"Man, where are these kids from?" says the Lieutenant.

"Oh, you think that's something," replies Corporal Keaty, "They've got moons and witches, and things that look like pumpkins. and these are suckers - but they're wrapped in some kind of clear paper. And it smells like sugar."

"Well Corporal," says the Lieutenant, "Take a bite."

Corporal Keaty takes a bite of Cubby's Halloween candy. "It's candy!" The lieutenant turns on the flashlight and looks in the bag, "This is impossible. Nobody can do this stuff. Corporal, you sure it's candy?"

"Oh yeah," replies the Corporal, "It's really good candy."

"Sergeant, let's see if we got this straight," says the Lieutenant, "I'm holding a container made of some mysterious substance that makes a light that's run from a battery looking in a bag of candy that's made to look like small witches and pumpkins and the moon. We're being visited by children, dressed in confederate

---

uniforms, that say they're from the future, and we're not supposed to be here - am I right?"

"Sir, yes, sir. I regret to inform you, Sir. That appears to be correct," answers the Sergeant.

"Private, take this bag down to the mill and give it to the kids," says the Lieutenant, "and see what they do with it. Sergeant - leave those weapons here by the fire, and take the horses back to the corral. Oh yeah, and Sergeant - check all water containers and make sure there's no alcohol in it."

"Sir, if I don't find any in the water," says the Sergeant, "may I have a drink?"

"If you don't find any in the water," replies the Lieutenant, "I think I'll have a drink with you. Well get going privates - get that bag of candy down there." Tommy and Johnny head by foot down to the mill with the strange new candy.

Tommy Miller is a nine year old farm boy from Rhode Island. He ran away from home with his cousin to join the army. Tommy has dreams of taking down the rebels with fierce bravado. He is reveling in camp life, and is eager to look good for the lieutenant. Johnny Swan, who is eleven, has become very close to Tommy. Johnny had been an orphan in a circus band. His circus had been traveling through Rhode Island when the war started. Being unhappy with the circus owner, he ran away from the circus to join the army. Johnny is nowhere near as rambunctious or war hungry as Tommy, and quite often finds his lips far too dry to blow his bugle. Johnny is quite ready to go

93

home. The kids travel through the night speculating on what the lieutenant had said, and how they had gotten in such a predicament. "Did you see the things the lieutenant has?" asks Johnny.

MAKING FRIENDS

(Chapter 13)

As Tommy and Johnny approach the mill, they can hear the four young confederate's conversation. Heather is afraid and starting to choke up, and Cody has his arm around her to console her. "We're in trouble," cries Heather. "We're in so much trouble."

"It's all right," replies Cody, "everything will be fine. This can't be happening; they're just pulling some kind of joke on us."

"Some kind of joke," retorts Sean.

"Time travel is not possible," responds Cody.

"Those rifles are real and loaded," says Cubby, "and those are not re-enactor's uniforms – they're the real thing. What would they be doing out here in the middle of the night? If it's a re-enactor's group, where is everyone else?"

"Ok, ok, it's Halloween," replies Cody. "There's got to be some reasonable explanation. You can't go back in time."

"I want to go home," replies Heather.

Cubby chimes in, "I'm hungry."

Hearing this, Tommy and Johnny enter into the mill. "Hi, I'm Tommy, and this is Johnny. What's Halloween?"

"What do you mean, what's Halloween?" responds Sean.

"Well, we've never heard of anything called Halloween," says Johnny.

"Oh, Halloween's great," answers Cubby, "We get dressed up in costumes and we go door to door and say trick-or-treat."

"Trick-or-treat?" says Johnny.

"Yeah, and they give us candy," answers Cubby.

"Oh – and I guess candy's the treat," says Tommy.

"Well – yeah."

"Well, what's the trick?" asks Tommy.

"You don't understand," responds Sean, "There is no real trick – it's just a saying."

"And I guess you say that the treats you get are what's in this sack," says Tommy.

"Oh, oh, I'm hungry," says Cubby. Tommy hands Cubby the bag, "Well the lieutenant says to give it to you, so here it is." Cubby grabs the bag, shoves his hand in, fills it with candy and begins to eat.

Johnny and Tommy look at Cubby and Johnny asks, "What is that you're eating?"

"Its candy," replies Sean, "Here have some. It's good." Sean reaches into the bag and hands them some of the candy. Johnny and Tommy cautiously take some of the candy. Johnny looks at Tommy as he slowly takes a bite.

Johnny gets a big smile on his face and says, "Its candy. It's good."

Tommy cautiously takes a bite and says, "Golly, I've never had anything like this. Where did you get this?"

Cubby replies, "Trick-or-treating."

"No, from the supermarket," retorts Sean.

—

"Supermarket?" asks Tommy.

"You know a grocery store," says Sean, "Or the drugstore."

"What's a grocery store?," asks Tommy.

"Oh you'd know it as a Mercantile," answers Heather remembering the word Mercantile on the sign at the Unison store.

"Where are you from?" asks Sean.

"What do you mean where are we from?" asks Johnny.

"You know," says Sean, "What town? What state?"

"Rhode Island," replies Tommy.

"Well, don't you all celebrate Halloween?" asks Sean.

"Well, I don't know what Halloween is," replies Tommy, "There are some people that celebrate All Hallows Eve."

"Well, All Hallows Eve has expanded into a bigger and national holiday called Halloween," says Sean. "It's kind of a fall festival and kids get dressed up as pirates, ghosts, witches, and characters. We're dressed up as soldiers."

"Aw – come on," says Johnny, "nobody is ever going to believe that."

"Well, look at the candy," says Sean, "look at the shapes they're in. Look at this. Do you know what a witch is?"

"Sure," says Tommy, "Witches are old hags with magical powers."

"Well, see," says Sean, "this candy is shaped like a witch that is flying on a broom."

"Witches or not," says Tommy, "nobody flies on a broom."

—

97

"It's just pretend," says Cubby.

"It's not real," says Heather, "like this whole situation. It's not real."

"Oh, yeah," replies Tommy, "we heard you talk about traveling in time. Nobody can go back in time. How stupid do you think we are?"

Cody hasn't spoken in a while and answers, "Well, that I can agree with you on nobody, can travel in time. So you can just stop clowning around and let us go home. Our parents are going to kill us."

"You aren't going nowhere but to a prison camp," responds Tommy.

Just then the Sergeant can be heard opening the door. He enters and beckons for Tommy to come meet him outside. The Sergeant hands Tommy the kid's equipment and asks him to find out how all of it works and what it's for. The Sergeant then heads back to camp, and Tommy brings everything into the mill. "I've been instructed to find out what this stuff is and how it works," says Tommy.

"I told you all," replies Cody, "It's a flashlight."

"What's a flashlight?" asks Tommy.

"It lights a light bulb with a battery," says Sean.

"What's a light bulb?" asks Tommy.

"You know," says Sean, "It's like a light bulb. You screw it into a light fixture, and turn the switch on. And it lights the house up. You've got to know what a light bulb is."

"What year is this?" asks Heather.

—

98

"You know what year it is," hollers Tommy.

"No," says Heather calmly, "what year is this?"

"It's 1862," says Johnny.

"No, it's 1982," replies Sean.

"Quit playing around," says Johnny."

It might be 1862 to you," says Sean, "but we're from 1982." All of the kids look at each other, baffled.

"All right," says Tommy, "if you're from 1982, how did you get here?"

"We don't know," says Heather, "we were just going metal detecting."

"What's metal detecting?" questions Tommy.

"We look for old stuff that soldiers would have left behind," says Cody.

"What stuff soldiers left behind," questions Tommy, "and what soldiers."

"Well, if this is really 1862," says Cody, "the stuff you all would have left behind."

"This doesn't make any sense," says Tommy.

"Ok," says Cody, "does this light make any sense?"

"Well, that's what we're here to find out," says Tommy. "We don't have anything like this - so how does it work?"

Cody asks, "Can I have the flashlight?"

"I guess so, here," responds Tommy handing over the flashlight.

—

"Come over by the fire," replies Cody, "and I will show you how this works." Cody takes the flashlight and unscrews the back to remove the batteries. He holds the battery up in the light, shows it to Tommy and Johnny and says, "This is a battery."

"That's not a battery," says Tommy.

"Do you know what electricity is?" asks Cody.

"I know what electricity is," replies Johnny, "Ben Franklin found it."

"Yeah," shouts Heather, "If this is 1862, you lit your house with coal, oil or gas, but we use electricity."

"Electricity is that little thing you call a battery?" questions Tommy.

"Well, in a way," says Sean. "It's stored electricity. Wait a minute and I'll show you." Sean takes the flashlight and unscrews the lens off of the front of the flashlight. He quickly removes the bulb, holds it up in the light, and says, "This is a light bulb."

Tommy takes the light bulb from Sean, looks at it and says, "How does this work?"

"If I take these two batteries and make it so that the batteries touch the light bulb, it makes the wires inside the glass glow."

Johnny takes the light bulb puts it up against the battery and replies, "This doesn't make it light up."

"I can't explain everything," says Sean, "But if you put the light bulb back into the flashlight, put the batteries back in and turn the switch on, it makes light."

100

"This doesn't make any sense," says Tommy.

"Have you ever been shocked?" asks Sean.

"No, we've never been shot," says Tommy.

"Not shot," answers Sean, "shocked. Stick your tongue on the end of the battery."

"I'm not sticking my tongue on anything," answers Tommy.

"It won't hurt you," says Cubby, "it won't hurt you – it just tingles. Look." Cubby takes the battery, sticks it on his tongue, shakes his head and makes a funny face.

"See," says Cubby.

"Oh give me that," says Johnny who proceeds to stick his tongue on the end of the battery. He feels a slight tingle in his jaw, which makes him step back in amazement. He hands the battery to Tommy.

Tommy looks at Johnny and says, "I'm not sticking my tongue on anything!"

"Oh give me that battery back," says Sean. Sean puts the flashlight back together, and turns it on, "See."

"That's electricity?" questions Tommy.

"It's just a little, tiny bit of electricity," answers Heather.

"So, you have these all through your house," asks Tommy, "lighting your house?"

"This is going to get crazy," says Sean. "So you say this is 1862. If this is 1862, a hundred years from now - from where we come from - there are ten million things that we have that you don't have. If this is 1862, you use a horse to get around or walk to wherever you go. We drive cars."

"What's a car?," asks Tommy.

"They're never going to believe this," replies Cubby.

"I can handle this one," says Heather. "You all have a wagon that the horses pull up the road. We get in a version of your wagon that has a motor in it that uses gasoline. You push on a pedal and it takes us up the road."

"Huh?" replies Tommy.

"Gas-O-Line?" asks Johnny.

"Gasoline?" asks Tommy, "What's gasoline?"

"Oh – oil," responds Cubby.

"Like the garbage that comes out of the ground?" Tommy asks.

"Yes and no," says Sean, "it's made from the oil that comes out of the ground."

"All right, so you have light run by electricity and a thing you call a car or a wagon that takes you from place to place. You have read too many science fiction books."

"Do you know about Jules Verne?" asks Cody.

"The playwright?" asks Tommy.

"Ok, well, I guess it's too early to connect this to Jules Verne," answers Cody, "but we have telephones, we have running water and plumbing, we have airplanes."

Tommy breaks in, "Airplanes?"

"Yeah," answers Sean, "we can fly."

Johnny starts laughing; "now you've got wings like birds."

"Well, yeah," replies Heather, "they do have wings."

"You have balloons," says Sean, "They fly."

"Well, yes, they go up and down," replies Tommy, "but they just move with the wind."

"If this is really 1862 about 30 years from now two brothers called the Wright Brothers will make a device called an airplane operated by the same motor that drives the car up and down the road, and in a few years you'll hear about Jules Verne," says Sean very proud of his scientific knowledge.

"Oh, balderdash," says Tommy. As the kids start to get closer and trust each other, they share the candy and talk about all of the amazing inventions that have been created over the past hundred and twenty years. Slowly but surely, taking every device they have, they explain everything to the two young soldiers. The two young soldiers start believing what Sean, Cody, Heather, and Cubby have said. The kids remove each modern device from their packs and try desperately to explain how and why they work. Now the original skepticism the two young soldiers had turned to amazement.

103

"You know, we may believe you," says Tommy, "but nobody else is going to, and you're in trouble."

"Can't you help us?" asks Heather.

"If we try to help you," answers Johnny, "the Sergeant will have our hides. Even if we did try to help you where would you go? How did you get here?"

"I don't know," replies Cody, "if we can just get back to the spot where we came from – maybe we can go back."

"Well, do you have a machine that can take you backwards and forwards in time?" asks Tommy.

"No! Nobody can travel in time," says Sean, "at least not yet."

"Well, how do you explain this?" asks Cody.

"I don't know," says Sean, "but I have a feeling that we shouldn't travel too far from here, or we'll get in worse trouble."

"We just can't let you go," replies Tommy.

"Please, our parents are going to kill us," says Heather.

"We could take them in the woods a ways," suggests Johnny.

"Oh, yes," replies Tommy, "and what do we tell the Sergeant? So you say that all the things you described we're going to have in a hundred years."

"Well, think of things that weren't around," says Sean, "just a few years ago, that you have now. There were no steam boats, there was no telegraph, there was no running water, there were no trains – there weren't even any cameras or pictures. In our world, we have movies."

"Oh golly day," says Tommy, "what are movies?"

"Well, you're really not going to believe this," says Sean, "but we have a box to look into that sends pictures that we watch for entertainment."

"Entertainment?" asks Johnny.

"Oh, oh," says Cubby reaching deep into his knapsack and pulling out a battery operated radio. He turns it on, and with amazement Tommy and Johnny fall back on their seats looking at the box as music emanates from it. Tommy gets up and comes close to the box peering at it, "I guess this works off of electricity, too."

All four kids answer at the same time, "Yes!"

"All right, all right," says Tommy, "I believe you. If for no other reason than we don't want to lose the war. We've got to get you out of here."

"You don't lose the war," says Sean, "you win the war."

"Oh, yes," replies Tommy, "now you can predict the future."

"I don't know how to explain any of this," says Sean. "Since you have said that you believe we're from 1982 – you have to know that we know who won the war."

Johnny, who has been listening to the strange music coming from the box finally chooses to speak, "That music is terrible. Where is it coming from? Turn that thing off before somebody hears it!" commands Tommy.

Heather says, "Guys, how can the radio be playing modern music if we're not in 1982?"

Sean says, "I can't explain being in 1862. How do you expect me to explain the radio?"

Tommy responds to the kids, "You all stay here for a little bit, and be quiet." Tommy signals to Johnny to step out the door.

Outside the mill Tommy says to Johnny, "How are we going to get them out of here?"

Johnny replies, "We're going to be in big trouble."

"Do you believe them?" asks Tommy.

"I don't know what to believe," responds Johnny, "but for some reason, I think we should help them."

"Do you think their soldiers?" asks Tommy.

"I can't explain it, but I believe they are who they say they are."

"So then, do we help them?" asks Tommy.

"Oh – the Sergeant is going to kill us," worries Johnny, "but, yes, we should help them."

PANIC

(Chapter 14)

A short distance away, a hundred and twenty years into the future, the Halloween celebration in Unison is coming to its conclusion. The mothers are packing the food up and putting away everything from the party at the church. Mr. Seaton and Mr. Craun enter the church overjoyed from their night of pranks on the children and the town. "Hey," says Mr. Craun to Mrs. Craun, "You can't believe the things we did to these kids."

"Oh, Ronnie," replies Mrs. Craun, "Won't you ever grow up. And speaking of kids, are they with you?"

"No – they came to the church hours ago," answers Mrs. Craun.

"We haven't seen those kids in hours," says Mrs. Seaton, "You better go look for them."

"Oh, they'll show up," says Mr. Craun.

"Ronnie Craun," answers Mrs. Craun, "It's eleven at night. Go find those kids."

Mr. Stuart enters into the church, "Hey, have you seen the kids? I've been all over this town."

"We were just talking about going to look for them," answers Mr. Seaton.

"Is the store locked up?" asks Mr. Stuart.

"No, Mrs. Connors is watching it," answers Mr. Seaton.

"Well, maybe they're at the house," says Mr. Craun.

"Ok, let's ride by the store," says Mr. Stuart, "and go by the house to see if they're there."

The three fathers proceed to the store to find Mrs. Connors getting ready to lock the store door. "Hey, Mrs. Connors," says Mr. Seaton. "Have you seen the kids?"

"No," says Mrs. Connors, "they haven't been here all night."

"Ok, keep the door unlocked in case they come back," says Mr. Seaton, "I still have the Halloween stuff to put away. Why don't you two go to the house to check for the kids, and I'll stay here to put the stuff away in case they show up here."

Mr. Craun and Mr. Stuart head to the Craun farmhouse. Mr. Craun busts into the house, "Hey mom are the kids here?"

"No, Ronnie," replies Grandma Craun, "Why don't you check the barn."

"They couldn't be in the barn," answers Mr. Stuart, "its pitch black."

"Well, they've got to be somewhere," says Mr. Craun, "so we'll check there and then head to your house." Mr. Craun and Mr. Stuart walk over to the barn and turn on the light.

"Heather, Sean, you in here," yells Mr. Stuart. Mr. Craun looks around the barn, enters the stalls and finds the horses gone.

"Uh, oh," says Mr. Craun, "those kids went riding."

"At night?" says Mr. Stuart, "No way, particularly Halloween night. Well, there's a piece of candy on the ground, and the horses are gone. They've been here."

"Those kids will break their fool necks, riding the horses across the pasture like that at night," answers Mr. Stuart.

"Maybe they went across the pasture to the church or to the store," says Mr. Craun.

"Ok, let's get back in the car and go to town," says Mr. Stuart. As they pull up to the store, Mr. Seaton is waiting at the door for them.

"Did you two take our machines? Did you go out without me?"

"Don't be so stupid," answers Mr. Craun. "We've all been in town."

"Well, I left those machines in the corner, and they're gone," replies Mr. Seaton, "Somebody has stolen our machines."

"Well, has the store been open?" asks Mr. Stuart.

"Well, yes and no, I've been at the store handing out candy," answers Mr. Seaton, "but at times I left the store to pull my pranks."

"The kids are missing and the horses are gone, too," replies Mr. Craun.

"Machines are gone, kids are missing, and horses are gone," thinks Mr. Seaton. "Those kids wouldn't possibly go metal detecting?"

"On Halloween night?" questions Mr. Stuart, "I know they want to go metal detecting, but its Halloween. Kids don't think about anything but trick-or-treating on Halloween night."

"Yeah," says Mr. Craun, "Maybe they rode over to the church." As the three fathers pull up to the church the mothers are locking the door.

"You got the kids?" asks Mrs. Stuart.

"No, we were hoping they were here," replies Mr. Stuart.

"Now don't get upset," says Mr. Craun reluctantly, "but the horses are missing from the barn."

"Oh, Ronnie, those kids will kill themselves riding alone at night," says Mrs. Craun, "What are they thinking?"

"Well, that's not the question," says Mr. Stuart. "The question is where those kids would go riding to at night?"

"That's not the question," says Mr. Seaton, "The question is why those kids would go riding at night?"

"Why don't you three go back to our house and see if they're there," says Mr. Stuart to the women. "Ronnie, you check the pasture from your house to the church, I'll take the car and ride towards Bloomfield and Seaton's Hill, and Doug you go back to the store and see if they show up. We'll meet back up at the Craun's, and if anybody finds them call Doug at the store."

Mr. Craun takes off on foot across the pasture. Mrs. Stuart, Mrs. Seaton, and Mrs. Craun drive to Mrs. Stuart's house, and Mr. Stuart drives up and down the country roads desperately trying to see in the field for any evidence of the four banshees. In the meantime, back at the store, Mr. Seaton starts to tear the store apart to see if he can find his metal detector. Appearing behind the counter, he looks down at General McCullen's map. Thinking back to a few days ago, he remembers that his map had been moved. He picks up the map and rolls it out. Inside he finds indentations in the paper, as if the map may have been traced. He rolls the map up and paces back and forth in the store in deep concentration. Muttering to himself he says, "Those kids really wanted to go metal detecting. They wouldn't do this."

About that time, Mr. Stuart pulls his car up in front of the store. Mr. Seaton hollers out to Mr. Stuart, "Did you find the kids?"

"No, I didn't find the kids," answers Mr. Stuart, "If I found the kids they'd be with me."

Slamming the door, he says to Mr. Seaton, "If I find those kids, I'm going to ring their necks."

"Did you trace General McCullen's map?" asks Mr. Seaton.

"No," replies Mr. Stuart.

"Well, somebody has."

"Have you talked to those kids about any of the places we've been metal detecting other than the valley below?" asks Mr. Stuart.

111

"Of course not," says Mr. Seaton, "There are too many live shells around." The phone rings behind the store counter, and Mr. Seaton picks it up to find Mrs. Stuart on the other line.

"Is my husband there?" asks Mrs. Stuart.

Yes, have you got the kids?" asks Mr. Seaton.

"No," replies Mrs. Stuart, "Are the kid's there?"

"No – the kids aren't here."

"Have you heard from Mr. Craun?" asks Mrs. Stuart.

"No," replies Mr. Seaton, "But John is here, and he didn't find them either."

"Oh no," says Mrs. Stuart.

"Well, we haven't heard from Ronnie yet," says Mr. Seaton, "Why don't you meet us back at the Crauns."

"Oh, Doug," worries Mrs. Stuart, "Where could those kids be?"

"I don't know, but don't worry they couldn't have gone far."

Mr. Seaton hangs up the phone, looks at Mr. Stuart and says, "Are you sure you haven't talked to those kids about any of the places we've been metal detecting."

Mr. Stuart replies, "I don't have to talk to the kids about where we've been metal detecting. They spy on us all the time."

"Well, the last time they were spying on us was the valley below. Maybe they went there." Mr. Stuart says to Mr. Seaton, "Oh, Doug its pitch black out there. Those kids are not going in that valley at night."

112

"Well, our machines are gone," replies Mr. Seaton, "someone's traced the map, the kids are gone, and the horses are gone. What do you think that means."

"I think we better get over to Ronnie's house in a hurry," answers Mr. Stuart. "Doug, they wouldn't do anything like that - not tonight."

"When you were their age, would you have done it?" asks Mr. Seaton.

"Yeah, but that's..." Mr. Stuart stops and thinks, "Oh boy." With that both fathers look at each other and bolt towards the car.

When they pull into the drive they find Mr. Craun with a flashlight across the road at the horse jump. Mr. Seaton rolls down his window and calls to Mr. Craun, "What are you doing?"

"Looking at hoofprints and dropped candy," answers Mr. Craun.

"What do you mean?" asks Mr. Seaton. "Hoofprints and dropped candy."

"Well Shadow has a distinct hoofprint," replies Mr. Craun, "There was four pieces of candy by the gate, three pieces of candy by the jump, and pieces of candy in hoofprints going across the field. What do you think it means?"

"Well, the machines are gone," says Mr. Stuart, "The maps traced, the kids are gone, the horses are gone, and the only way to have had candy is to go trick-or-treating first."

Mr. Seaton looks at Mr. Craun, "Have you talked to those kids about any place we went metal detecting?"

Mr. Stuart says slyly, "How about a place we haven't been metal detecting?"

Mr. Seaton, Mr. Craun and Mr. Stuart all say together, "Mountsville!"

"You were talking about metal detecting at the battle of Mountsville fought on Halloween night," says Mr. Stuart to Mr. Seaton.

"Oh, oh, they wouldn't," says Mr. Seaton. "They're stealing our camp! And at night? They wouldn't."

"Well, we can't follow in the car," says Mr. Stuart.

"Gentlemen, mount up!" commands Mr. Craun. The three men hurriedly proceed to the barn and start to saddle some horses. The three mothers pull into the drive thoroughly panicked, as the three men are coming out of the barn leading the horses.

"Have you got the kids?" asks Mrs. Craun, "And what are you doing?"

"We don't have time to explain," says Mr. Craun, "I need you to call the police and the fire department. Get out a search party."

Then Mr. Stuart says, "After you call the police and get a search party started, one of you drive a car up the road towards Pothouse. One of you can drive up the Unison Road. The other group drives up the St Louis Road. Proceed towards Snickersville Turnpike."

Mrs. Stuart who is totally panicked and frustrated answers, "Will you please speak in modern language? What's the Snickersville Turnpike?"

"Oh, Route 628, Route 611, and Route 734," replies Mr. Stuart. As the fathers swing up onto the saddles, digging their heels into the horse's sides, lunging across the road, jumping the horse jump, the mothers scream out, "Where are you going?"

Mr. Craun bellows back, "Across country… See you in Mountsville."

Mrs. Craun screams, "Where's Mountsville?"

"Goose Creek Bridge," yells Mr. Stuart, "Route 734." At a full gait the fathers cross the pasture reeling their horses. Using a flashlight they peer down at the ground looking for candy.

At a break neck pace, Mr. Stuart looks at them, "We're going to kill ourselves."

"We can go as fast as we can now," says Mr. Craun, "but look at that fog over there. We're going to have to slow up anyway."

THE GREAT ESCAPE

(Chapter 15)

Back at the camp, Johnny says to Tommy, "I want you to go to the corral and get their horses."

"How?" asks Tommy.

"I don't know," replies Johnny, "but we need to get their horses to them. Most likely there's not going to be a guard there this time of night anyway. If there is a guard, tell them the lieutenant said to get the horses. You take those horses, and get them out of the back side of the camp, unseen. You know the deep ravine – way back in the woods?" Tommy nods. "Take the horses there, and somehow I'll try to get the kids past the picket to the ravine," says Johnny. Johnny ducks back into the mill, looks at the kids and says, "I'm going to be gone for a while. Be quiet. If somebody shows up while I'm gone tell them the Sergeant called for us, and that's all you know." Johnny walks toward the outside picket on the back side of the camp. As he gets close to the picket, Johnny is peering through the woods, sees that the picket is half asleep and leaning on his rifle. Johnny heads back to the camp and he sees a smaller ravine. He thinks that he can use this to get the kids around the picket without being seen.

Johnny returns to the mill, steps in and tells the four kids, "Follow me and keep quiet." The four kids follow Johnny through the woods into the small ravine. They sneak by the pickets trying not to make any noise. Cubby trips over a branch, causing the rest of the group to freeze in fear. A picket hears the noise and commences to look around through the trees in the forest, but not finding anything he returns to his post. Heather is shaking and almost visibly in tears.

Cody looks at Cubby and whispers, "Cubby, for once in your life, stop being clumsy." Johnny looks at them all and whispers urgently, "For God's sake, stay quiet!" The four banshees and the young bugler stealthfully proceed through the woods to the large bank overlaying the large ravine. The kids slide down the bank into the large ravine, and quietly wait for Tommy to arrive with the horses.

Within a few moments, a large ruffling and the sound of hooves can be heard coming from the other side of the ravine. "Johnny, Johnny!" says Tommy, "When I was leaving with the horses, I saw the Sergeant heading towards the mill."

"Oh, oh, we've got to go back," says Johnny, "we've got to go back."

"What about the horses?" asks Tommy?

"Leave them Leave them," answers Johnny, "tie them up."

"What if they find the horses gone?" asks Tommy.

117

"Tie those horses up. We've got to get back to the mill before the Sergeant gets there." Heather cries, "Please don't take us back."

"We've got to," answers Johnny. "We got out once we can do it again. The whole camp will be on alert."

"What's the difference?" hollers Tommy, "We're in so much trouble now – we'll be in just as much trouble then."

"We're not deserting," commands Johnny. We're going back to the mill now." Johnny starts to push the four kids up the embankment, when at that moment three large reports of artillery echo through the woods and the night sky lights up with massive flashes of light. The force of the explosion throws the kids back into the bottom of the ravine. With only a momentary lull, two more loud explosions with flashes can be seen coming from the direction of the main camp. Tommy says to Johnny, "We're under attack!" Johnny looks at the kids and retorts, "You are spies!"

Cody looks at Johnny and answers, "We're not spies!"

Johnny looks at Tommy and commands, "We've got to get back. We've got to get back now. You kids stay here." With that Johnny and Tommy try to scramble up the embankment walls, but Cody grabs Johnny and says, "What are you thinking - you're going to get killed." Johnny pushes Cody down to the ground hard and climbs up the embankment running away through the woods.

The next thing the kids hear is Johnny blowing his bugle playing the call to arms. At the same time, the sharp report of musket fire tears through the woods and the kids hear the screams of command from the Union Officers and the Rhode Island Volunteers. The kids brace themselves for the assault knowing that it must be General Stuart's Confederate Calvary coming to attack the Rhode Island regiment. For the next ten minutes, the kids huddle down in the ravine shivering from the bite of the night's air and fear of being killed. As the battle rages, the ground vibrates and the musket balls screech through the air breaking the limbs off of trees. Cries of wounded soldiers can be heard echoing through the woods. The confederate's high pitched rebel yell can be heard in the distance. The pounding of horses hooves can be felt as General Stuart's Cavalry charges across the road and into the Union camp forcing the Union soldiers to break and run.

There is now chaos as the Union Army seems to be running in all directions. Johnny slides down the embankment, "You kids have got to run. Get out of here." Before any of the kids have time to think, two other Union soldiers slide down the embankment to avoid enemy fire and come face to face with our four confederate banshees. There is a moment of fear and silence as none of them knows how to react. The Union soldiers scramble up the embankment and scurry away into the forest.

As this is happening, a Confederate Calvary man on a fierce horse appears at the top of the embankment.

Cubby looks up to see his father, "Dad!" cries Cubby. The man on the horse rears the horse back looking into Cubby's eyes. A puzzled look appears on his face as he wheels his horse around, raises his saber, digs his spurs into the flank of the horse and commands his horse to jump the embankment disappearing back into the battle.

THE RESCUE

(Chapter 16)

The three fathers galloped across the fields entering the dense fog. It becomes precariously harder for them to see where they're going and for their horses to find their footing on the ground. "Ronnie," Doug says, "this is impossible. We've got to go down by the creek."

"Well, let's hope the kids went that way," answers Mr. Craun, "but no matter what we'll have to follow the creek downstream to get through." The fathers entered the ravine seeing off in the distance, a large yellow light.

"What is that?" asks Mr. Stuart.

"It can't be a house," says Mr. Craun, "It's too much light."

"It's a campfire," says Mr. Seaton, "glowing in the fog."

"What would a campfire being doing out here in the middle of the night?" asks Mr. Stuart.

"I don't know," says Mr. Seaton, "but no farmer would be burning trash out here in the middle of the night. That's one big fire." The three fathers spurred their horses on down the creek. Mr. Seaton comes to the ford, looks down and sees a piece of candy. Mr. Seaton dismounts, picks up the piece of candy and lights his flashlight into the ground.

There are tracks of four horses and at least ten people on the ground, "Ronnie, look at this."

"Well, that's Shadow's hoofprint," replies Mr. Craun.

"Yeah, and look at all these other prints," answers back Mr. Seaton.

"Well, they crossed the ford here," says Mr. Craun. He crosses the ford and the deep cut of the road embankment. He looks off to the right of the road to a high embankment and sees the last embers of a glowing campfire. Mr. Craun walks his horse up the embankment to the dying campfire and takes his flashlight shining it around. There lying on the ground, he sees a civil war musket.

"John, Doug, come here." Both of them pull their horse up the hill finding Mr. Craun holding a civil war musket. "Look at this – What the heck?" Mr. Seaton looks around and finds a clay pipe, still warm.

"You know," says Mr. Stuart, "if I didn't know any better, I would say this is a picket post."

"Oh – maybe somebody is hunting," says Mr. Craun.

Mr. Seaton holds up the pipe, "With a clay pipe and a musket with a bayonet on it? This is weird," says Mr. Stuart, "This is really getting weird. We need to get to the Unfrequented Road."

"I'm taking this rifle," says Mr. Craun.

"Leave it," retorts Mr. Seaton, "We can come back for it." The men mount their horses and trot out into the field.

"You feel like we're being watched?" asks Mr. Seaton.

"Doug!" cries Mr. Stuart, "Don't start."

"Why don't we scout around for a moment," says Mr. Craun, "I'll go to the left towards the big light in the fog. Doug, you go ahead and scurry around to see if you can pick up the kid's tracks. John you go to the right and check out the edge of the woods. We'll all meet back here in a few minutes. Doug, if you pick up the tracks of the kids, you holler out. John, if you pick up the tracks of the kids, you holler out. If I pick up the tracks of the kids, I'll holler out."

With that, the three fathers spur their horses and move across the wide pasture. Mr. Stuart reaches the wood line and commences to walk his horse up the side of the woods. Peering through the thick woods, he sees a shadowy glimpse of a silhouette running through the trees. He spurs his horse to come up more even with the silhouette. He stops in amazement as the moon allows him to see in full view, a Union soldier, dressed in full gala crossing into a small clearing and then darting back into the woods. "Hey, you!" Mr. Stuart stops and thinks better of what he just did, "That just can't be. I know I just saw a soldier." Wheeling his horse, he spurs his horse to a gallop and heads toward the center of the field.

At the same time, Mr. Craun was galloping his horse towards a large hazy light way to the left side of the field. As he peered off into the distance, shadowy figures start to appear. Pulling his horse up to a walk, he slowly approaches the figures as they become more visible. In disbelief of what he thinks he sees, he pulls his horse to a stop, dismounts, and slowly approaches the light. He is amazed to see a large confederate picket post.

"Well, I don't believe it," says Mr. Craun to himself, "but I'm not going up there by myself." Taking his horse and walking it back a safe distance where he knows he can't be seen, he mounts his horse, digs his spurs in and charges at a full gallop towards the center of the field. In the meantime, Mr. Seaton had picked up the trail of the four banshees finding candy and hoofprints in the ground. Mr. Seaton mounts his horse and moves at a quick gait across the field till he enters the Unfrequented Road. Looking off in the distance, where the road enters the tree line, he pulls his horse up in amazement as he swears he sees the last of a confederate cavalry column on the road entering the woods. Spinning his horse around, he gallops to the center of the field. Mr. Seaton dismounts and bends down to find trampled pieces of candy. Mr. Craun and Mr. Stuart, come charging across the field and pull up to Mr. Seaton who is picking up a piece of candy off of the ground.

"Doug," says Mr. Craun, "You're not going to believe what I just saw."

"Oh no," retorts Mr. Stuart, "You're not going to believe what I just saw."

"Let me guess," answers Mr. Seaton, "You saw confederate soldiers. Am I right?"

"Doug, I swear," says Mr. Craun, "I just saw a large confederate picket post silhouetted by a large fire."

"I just saw a Union soldier running through the woods," says Mr. Stuart.

"Yeah, and I just saw a full Confederate Cavalry column," retorts Mr. Seaton. "Now, who believes in ghosts."

"There is no reason for re-enactors being out here," says Mr. Craun.

"Well, I don't know if any of us is getting spooked by this night or what we think we're seeing," answers Mr. Seaton, "but there is no denying that there are hundreds of horse tracks on this ground and smashed candy." Mr. Stuart and Mr. Craun dismount and bend down to look on the ground.

"What do you think those kids have gotten into?" asks Mr. Stuart. At that moment, off in the distant, three large reports of artillery fire can be heard causing the horses to panic.

The men grab the reins to control their horses, and all three men say, "Whoa." They look off in the distance to hear two more reports of artillery and see large flashes of light through the woods.

"This can't be," hollers Mr. Stuart.

"Well, Doug, you always wanted to go metal detecting and see what happens at the actual time of the battle," says Mr. Craun, "Looks like you're going to get your chance."

"You think that they've got our kids?" worries Mr. Seaton.

"This can't be happening," says Mr. Stuart. "There's no such thing as ghosts!" With that, the crack of musket fire can be heard distinctly and the sounds of the rebel yell echoes through the valley.

"Mount up! Mount up! Mount up!" cries Mr. Seaton.

"What the hell do you think we're going to do?" yells Mr. Stuart.

"Ride to hell gentlemen," answers Mr. Craun. "Looks like we're riding to hell!" The three men with a running mount, swing up onto their horses. Digging their heels into their horses, spurring on to a full charge, across the field and onto the Unfrequented Road, they dash up the road into the woods as the battle sounds and lights of engagement fully encompass their senses. The ground vibrates with each report of artillery.

"Oh my, Holy Toledo," cries Mr. Craun, "We're all gonna die!"

"It's too late now," retorts Mr. Seaton, "keep on going." A confederate soldier steps out into the road and points his rifle at the three men hollering "Halt!" The three horses rush by pushing the confederate soldier aside. The bullets whizz by their ears breaking tree limbs all around them. The three men grab onto the horses' manes and crunch down to avoid the bullets. They cross the crest of a hill in the road and come down a steep embankment. They come across a horse jump in their path, which forces them to jump over it. The horses slide down the hill from the momentum of the jump into the road where they are greeted by brilliant lights flashing red and the sound of sirens. The police cars, ambulances and fire engines pull up almost hitting the three fathers' on their horses. The men pull their horses around in a circle trying to orient them to what is going on.

Mr. Stuart gets off his horse and hollers, "Oh, my gosh. What just happened?"

Mrs. Stuart comes running up out of her car, "Did you find the kids? Did you find the kids?"

"I don't know," answers Mr. Seaton, "I don't know. Wait a minute." Then, from behind the fire engines, comes the sound of Cubby's voice, "Dad, dad, dad!" The parents run toward the sound to find their respective children.

Mrs. Stuart grabs Heather and pulls her into her arms, "What were you thinking? You could have been hurt or killed."

"Oh, mom," cries Heather, "You don't know how right you are."

"Dad, dad," cries Cubby. "You were in the Confederate Cavalry?"

"Cubby," Mrs. Seaton answers. "There is going to be no TV. You are in such trouble."

"Mom," says Sean, "You're not going to believe this. I know you're not going to believe this, but we just went back in time."

"The only time you're going to be thinking about," answers Mrs. Stuart, "is the time you're going to be spending in your room."

"Look, I think we all need to calm down," says Mr. Stuart, "We can discuss this when we get home. You get these kids in the car and you get them home."

A policeman walks up to Mr. Craun and asks, "Mr. Craun, do you mind telling me what is going on here, please?"

"Well, I don't know if I can explain it to you," replies Mr. Craun, "And I'm not sure that you would believe me, if I told you." Mr. Seaton looks up the hill, and sees the burning embers of a fire up in the woods, "Look," he indicates to where the fire is. The fathers and the two policemen head up to the fire pit. They look around the fire pit and find their metal detectors, and hanging on the handle of one of the metal detectors is a Union Soldier capy hat. Mr. Seaton grabs the hat and shows it to the other two fathers. Mr. Stuart opens the cap and finds a note folded into its band. He opens the note and shines the flashlight onto it. He reads,

*An artifact for my four young
confederate friends.
Evidently, lost in time.
Signed Sergeant O'Grady, First Rhode
Island Cavalry*

Mr. Stuart hands the note to the policeman, "Well, believe it or not, this is what appears have happened." The three fathers take the capy and slide up onto their horses. They grab the reins of the remaining horses and start to pull away in a slow gait up the road.

"Wait wait," cries the policeman, "What am I supposed to write in my report?"

Mr. Seaton looks back and says, "Just what the note says: Four young confederate banshees lost in time." The three fathers slowly walk up the road without saying a word. They come to Carter's plantation gate, and on the gate they find a large sign:

"It's Halloween. No way are we staying here. No trick-or-treaters."

RETRIBUTION

(Chapter 17)

The next few days for our four Confederate banshees could be said to be at the very least – very uncomfortable, but nowhere near as it was uncomfortable for their fathers. The more the dads and the kids tried to convey what had happened to them, the less their mothers cared to hear about what they believed to be a tall tale. As far as their moms were concerned, their dad's hobby had threatened their children's safety. Furthermore, their father's over enthusiasm for all things that had happened over a hundred years ago had infiltrated into their family's lives far too much. In the words of Mrs. Stuart, "I do not want to hear one more word about anything involving the Civil War, ever, period." The father's, on the other hand, could not believe what they believed occurred and could hardly retain themselves from digging deeper into the mystery of that night. The fathers drove to Mountsville and walked over the ground. There was no evidence of any camp or fire pit. They walked the Unfrequented Road till they had almost convinced themselves that what they thought had happened was just their imagination.

Standing at the counter of Unison Store a few days later, Mr. Stuart says, "There is no such thing as ghosts." But Mr. Seaton gives his usual sly grin, reaches under the counter, and pulls out the Union capy.

He opens the hat rim, removes the note from within the rim, and throws it on the counter, "Well, what about this?"

"You know," says Mr. Craun, "We need to talk to those kids."

"I don't know about you," says Mr. Stuart, "but if I even get near my own kids and start to have a conversation about the Civil War, I won't be married anymore. Doug, why don't you talk to Cubby?"

Mr. Seaton answers, "Well, Cubby keeps insisting that I was dressed as a Confederate soldier, and his mom wants us both to talk to a psychiatrist."

"Well, that leaves you, Ronnie," replies Mr. Stuart.

"Look," says Mr. Craun, "Cody is not saying a word, and Ma Craun and my wife are hovering around him like eagles protecting their young."

"What the heck?" says Mr. Stuart, "They're our kids, too."

"Yeah, right," answers Mr. Craun. We should have taken those kids metal detecting a long time ago.

Mr. Seaton chimes in, "Just let it quiet down for a while. Besides, I think we need to talk to all four of them together."

"By the way, Doug," asks Mr. Stuart, "How did you get that note anyway? I thought you gave it to the policeman."

"I have connections and friends," retorts Mr. Seaton, "and it's a good thing, too, or we would have been down at the police station trying to explain all of this."

"Well, why aren't we?" asks Mr. Stuart.

"As the state police said to me," answered Mr. Seaton, "it never happened. Just let it go. It never happened. Period."

It was about three weeks later when the four Confederate banshees finally began to have a more normal life. Between school, punishment and chores, all had been purposefully kept busy. Every time they could get together, they would talk about their Halloween adventure.

The kids were sitting on the school bus analyzing their gruesome night on the way to school one morning. "That was dad, right?" states Cubby, "That was my dad?"

Cody answers, "Cubby, I didn't get a good look at him."

"I did," said Heather, "It was Mr. Seaton."

"I told you," retorts Cubby.

"Maybe it was one of their tricks," answers Sean.

"Are you kidding?" replies Cody.

Heather states, "No one can go back in time."

"Look, not even our fathers are this good at playing tricks," says Sean, "I don't understand, but we just need to forget about it."

"When are we going to be able to get together again to go out metal detecting?" asks Heather.

"Are you kidding?" asks Sean, "We still haven't gotten to go metal detecting."

"You are nuts," replies Cody to Heather, "I've had enough of trying to go metal detecting."

"It was a little hairy," replies Heather, "but it was a really neat evening of adventure."

Cody answers, "I don't know about you, but my mother's really mad. I can barely get out of my room let alone go metal detecting in the woods. Furthermore, I'm tired of all of these chores."

"You're tired of all of these chores," says Sean, "I bet your mother's nowhere near as mad as our mother."

"Mom wants me to see a doctor," chimes in Cubby.

"How's Shadow, Cody?" asks Heather.

"I don't know?" answers Cody, "Part of my punishment is that I'm not allowed near the horses. Grandpa takes care of them."

"They can't stay mad forever," answers Sean.

"I don't know," says Heather, "Mom's really been giving it to dad. Well, as soon as this flies over, I say we meet at the barn and make plans to go back."

Sean and Cody holler, "No way!" "
I don't even want to talk about it anymore," replies Sean.

"Suit yourself," answers Heather.

The week of Thanksgiving the three mothers can be found at Ma Crauns preparing the food for the Thanksgiving feast at the church. Ma Craun broke down first about letting the kids off of their severe punishment, "Young ladies, it's about time for those kids to take care of those horses. Pa can't do it much longer, and those horses need to be exercised. Besides, we're sitting here getting ready for the coming Thanksgiving services at church, and I'm getting a little tired of all of this tension and anxiety," says Ma Craun, "Why don't you let them go riding in the pasture."

"Oh, ok girls," says Mrs. Craun, "What do you think?"

"All right," says Mrs. Stuart, "if it's ok with the two of you."

"Well, I might let these kids off," answers Mrs. Seaton, "but if you think I'm letting Doug off the hook, you're crazy. I think he needs to go see a psychiatrist."

"Well, if he goes," says Mrs. Stuart, "make sure John and Ronnie go with him."

"Ma," said Mrs. Craun, "do you know how much trouble they've caused. Have you listened to their story?"

"I know, I know," says Ma Craun, "but you've got to give them a lot of credit for their imagination."

"What if it wasn't imagination?" asks Mrs. Seaton.

Mrs. Stuart responds, "There is no such thing as ghosts."

"You can't keep these kids apart and locked up forever," replies Grandma.

The next Saturday, the four confederate banshees could be found at the barn saddling their horses, but no one was very talkative.

Mr. Craun walks into the barn and says, "Hey, kids! Why so glum?"

Patting Shadow on her side Cody says, "Oh, dad. - Are we crazy?"

"I don't think so," says Mr. Craun. "Why don't you kids ride your horses across the pasture over to the store, and tie them up there. You can have some soda and some treats."

"What about mom?" asks Cody.

"Don't worry about it," answers Mr. Craun, "but be quiet and don't tell anyone."

"Dad," Cody tries to ask a question, but Mr. Craun cuts him off, "It'll be all right. I'll meet you at the store.

A short time later, the four kids find their fathers waiting for them at the store. "Hey, kids," says Mr. Seaton, "Want a soda and someone to tell your Halloween story to?"

Cubby not able to contain himself any longer answers, "Dad, did you pull a trick on us, or were you in the Civil War?"

"Cubby, I promise you I was not in the Civil War," replies Mr. Seaton, "but we've been thinking about this." Mr. Seaton reaches under the counter and pulls out a book about John Mosby's Rangers. He opens the book to a marked page with a picture of Mosby's Rangers and says, "Does he look familiar?

———

"Yeah," answers Cubby, "that's you dad - That's him! See he was in the Civil War."

"So who is that?" asks Sean.

Mr. Seaton replies, "It's Cubby's great, great grandfather."

"Holy Toledo," says Heather, "Mr. Seaton, you look just like your great grandfather."

"You're trying to tell us we went back into time?" asks Sean.

"We don't know," answers Mr. Stuart, "we don't know! Why don't you kids just tell us what happened." For the next hour the four kids exuberantly conveyed their story to their fathers. The fathers listened, laughed and took in their story as if they had just read it out of the official records of the war of the rebellion.

"Well, dad," asks Cody, "Do you think we're crazy?" Mr. Seaton gives off his big grin, reaches under the counter and pulls out the Union capy. He opens the hat brim, removes the note, and slyly says, "Have you met a Sergeant O'Grady?"

"Yes, you did pull a trick on us," says Cody defiantly.

"No," says Mr. Craun, "This capy was left for the four of you. See what the note says:

An artifact for my four young
confederate friends.
Evidently, lost in time.
Signed Sergeant O'Grady, First Rhode
Island Cavalry

———

"Now what do you think?"

"I don't know," says Cody.

"We're going metal detecting," says Mr. Stuart, "Want to come?"

"What about mom?" asks Sean.

"What mom doesn't know won't hurt her, will it?" replies Mr. Stuart.

"Where?" asks Heather, "Can we go to Mountsville?"

"Oh no," says Mr. Seaton, "not there. We're going to drive over to Beaver Dam Creek. Want to come along?"

"Yes," answers Heather.

"I don't know," says Cubby sheepishly.

"Aw, it'll be fun," answers Heather.

"Aren't you even a little bit cautious?" asks Cody.

"This is my sister you're talking to," answers Sean. The fathers laugh.

After a short ride, the four kids and the fathers get out of the truck. The dad's hand the metal detectors to the kids. "Why don't you all scramble up that bank," says Mr. Craun, "and see if you can find anything around that tree." The four kids scurry up the hill, and within moments can be heard the familiar beep of their father's metal detectors.

"Dad, dad!" says Cubby, "We got something."

Mr. Seaton hollers back up from the bottom of the hill, "Well, dig it up." The four kids are beside themselves from the excitement of their first find.

"What you got?" asks Mr. Stuart.

137

"It's a rifle or a musket barrel," answers Cody.

"Really?" replies Mr. Seaton, "Got the trigger assembly and hammer yet?"

"How about a bayonet?" asks Mr. Craun. The kids run back to the truck with their newly found artifact.

"Dad," asks Cody, "How did you know where to look?"

"Well son," replies Mr. Craun, "It appears Mr. Stuart now believes in ghosts."

Mr. Stuart says, "You kids weren't the only ones who had an adventure. Wait until we tell you our story. Come on let's go home before we get into trouble."

"Can't we look some more?" asks Heather.

"Believe us kids," says Mr. Stuart, "We won't go metal detecting without you – anymore."

"Yeah right," whispers Cody to Heather under his breath.

THE END

Carter Family House

The Modern Day
Goose Creek.
Old stone bridge torn down.

The Rhode Island Camp and Battle Above Snickersville Turnpike

The Horse Jump at Mountsville
Above Snickersville Turnpike

The Unfrequented Road
To Mountsville

Mountsville Country Store

Muskets
To Your
Left

Ford and Picket
At Beaver Dam Creek

South Fork
FRIENDS BURYING GROUND
1771

Confederate Banshees Beware!! Ha! Ha!

No Camping

Unison Store
As It Appears Today

Union Church with the pencil graffiti on the walls

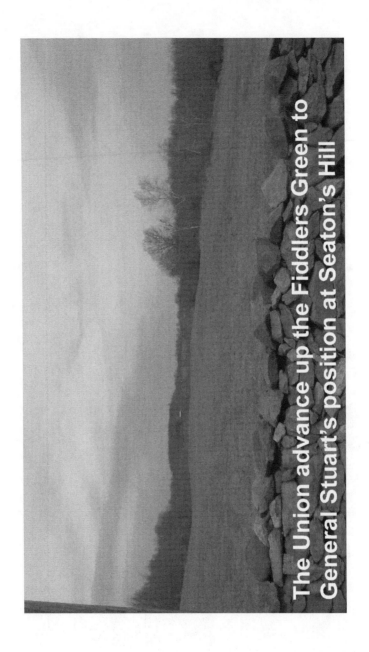

The Union advance up the Fiddlers Green to General Stuart's position at Seaton's Hill

Yankees to my left
Rebels to my front
Seaton's Hill
The rock lined road

Horse jump at Seaton's Hill

General Stuart's position at Seaton's Hill

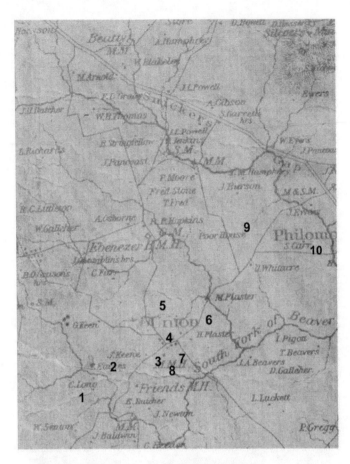

1-Seaton's Hill   2-Fiddlers Green
3-Unison Church   3-Unison Store
5-Pelham's Artillery Redoubt
6-Valley Below   7-Craun Farm
8-Grave Yard
9-First Contact & Engagement Battle of Union, VA
10-Beaver Dam Creek & Ford

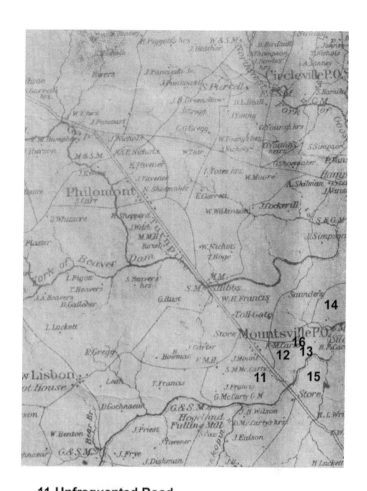

11-Unfrequented Road
12-Horse Jump
13-Rhode Island Camp
14-Mill
15-Goose Creek Bridge
16-Carter House

About The Authors

Larry Portch lived in the Middleburg VA area, located in Loudoun County, for many years and had a high interest in the history of the Civil War and metal detecting. Most of his story was pieced together from his exploits and research on the subject.

Michelle Portch was an actress and drama teacher having a Master's Degree in theatrical and technical arts from San Diego State University. She has listened to her father's tales most of her life and encouraged and helped him write this tale.

9665904R0009

Made in the USA
Charleston, SC
01 October 2011